The Wonders of Vale

Modern Magick, 7

Charlotte E. English

1

Betrayal.

It hurts when your enemies do it, but at least you expect them to stab you in the back at every available opportunity.

It's six times as bad when it's your friends. Miranda being approximately my least favourite person on the planet at this time, I... am not in any hurry to work with her again.

Unfortunately, Milady insists.

This is why she's the boss and I'm the lackey. She was no more impressed than the rest of us when Miranda defected to Ancestria Magicka, indulging in a spot of espionage (at our expense) on her way out. As far as I'm concerned, Miranda's dead to me, whatever her skills may be, or however useful her particular brand of expertise.

But Milady sees opportunity, and takes it. The job must be finished, progress must be made, and if we need Miranda then we need Miranda.

I just wish she'd sent someone other than me to arrange it.

Ah well. If wishes were unicorns, lots of people other than my good self would ride them, and that's just a messy prospect.

As for her probable location, well, I did some subtle asking around. And when I say "subtle" I mean I put posters up in all the common rooms and corridors at Home, emblazoned with Miranda's picture and the words: HAVE YOU SEEN THIS WOMAN?

Hey, I'm taking leaves out of Milady's book. Whatever gets the job done.

Anyway, it didn't take all that long to establish that I am in fact the last member of the Society who's known to have had contact with Miranda. I'd suspected as much.

I'd last seen her on the fifth Britain, in the halls of the transplanted Ashdown Castle. It hadn't been an easy conversation, but fortunately it hadn't been a lengthy one either. Miranda had brought my pup back to me, which had won her back one or two measly points of my esteem (current balance: minus nine hundred and ninety-nine thousand, nine hundred and ninety-eight).

And that was that. Where she had gone afterwards, I simply had no idea. Had she been part of the group of Society and Ancestria Magicka members we'd forcibly hauled back to the sixth? Had she made it back here, somehow, on her own?

Or was she still there?

I felt in my heart that she was still on the fifth. The allure of the place affected all of us; I'd practically had to drag Jay back by his hair, and I don't know anybody more devoted to his family than he.

Meanwhile, we've reason to believe that the fifth is absolutely crawling with magickal beasts — the kind that are, at best, highly endangered in our Britain, and at worst outright extinct. The kinds of creatures Miranda would sell her grandmother to gain access to (or her friends, allies and employer, because sure, *what are we worth anyway?*)

Ahem. As I said, Miranda would want to stay.

So said my heart. Course, my heart has a bad habit for talking utter crap, so what do I know?

'How do you feel about gut instincts?' I said to Jay.

He looked up at me, blinking with the dazed look of a man so deeply engrossed by a book as to be having trouble finding his way out of it again. We were in our favourite spot in the first floor common room, tucked into chairs by the longest window. I had a stack of five books balanced on the arm of my chair. Jay had twelve.

'Context?' he said.

'Detective work.'

'Aha, you mean a good old-fashioned hunch.'

'I've a hunch Miranda's still on the fifth Britain.'

'I've a hunch you might be right.'

'Two hunches make a...'

'Spectacular lack of evidence.'

I sighed, and slouched deeper into my chair. I'd sent Miranda a slew of messages, of course; I still had her number. She hadn't answered any of them. Was that because she didn't want to talk to me, or because she was too far beyond reach to receive any of them?

We were waiting for one of two things to happen: either a summons from the great Orlando, genius inventor, who reportedly had a stash of new toys for us to play with; or the arrival of our promised help from Mandridore, which may or may not include Baron Alban.

I'd had trouble focusing on any of the several books I'd purloined from the library. Good, improving reads, all of them, but I was restless and distracted and it was all I could do to stay in my seat. I'd got up twice and paced about, but trailing aimlessly from window to window doesn't pass the time as effectively as you might think, considering its popularity as an activity.

When at last I heard footsteps approach, the brisk kind that heralded someone on a mission, I hurled aside my book with a carelessness that would've turned Val's stomach, and launched myself out of my chair.

It was Indira.

'Yes?' I said, beaming.

'Orlando's ready to see you,' she said to me, with her customary politeness.

Jay didn't look up from his book.

'Hey, big brother,' I said, poking him.

He looked up. 'Huh?'

'You're up, Jay,' said Indira, and she more or less meant this literally, since Orlando's secret lair is in the attics.

'Right.' Jay rose with considerably more composure than I had contrived to display, and set his book aside with all the tender care I should've employed.

Does nothing rattle this man? Honestly.

I confess to experiencing more than a little excitement. I scarcely exaggerate when I refer to Orlando's workshops as super-secret. Few people are allowed in there; Indira's one of the very rare exceptions, and she's only permitted because she's a genius too, and Orlando's training her as his assistant.

Everyone else? Forget it.

Even me.

When Milady had told us to "report to Orlando", I'd assumed she meant he would arrange to have our new stuff delivered by somebody... not him. He's a recluse, like most geniuses, and I've set eyes on him exactly twice in my entire history with the Society.

But no. We'd been sent to the common room, there to await Orlando's personal summons. *Personal.*

I wanted to take it as a compliment to Jay and I, but no. Orlando didn't work like that. Rather, it was evidence of the importance Milady placed upon our particular mission. To get this job done, we all had to step up and do things we hated: Jay and I had to deal with Miranda, and Orlando had to deal with people in general.

As we followed Indira up and up the winding stairs to the attics, I resolved upon being as normal and unalarming as possible. Halfway up the stairs, I surreptitiously adjusted the hue of my hair. Bright pink might be taken amiss by a man of shy habits; perhaps a soothing shade of russet might be more appropriate.

Jay gave me a funny look.

'What?' I said, hiding the hand that wore my colour-changing ring behind my back.

'What are you doing?'

'Last-minute emergency personality recalibration.'

'Why?'

'I don't want to startle the genius.'

Jay's eyes registered amusement, but his face remained perfectly grave. 'I liked the pink.'

'It did go nicely with this dress,' I allowed, glancing down at the cream silk confection I was wearing.

'Geniuses are notoriously eccentric, you know.'

He had a point.

By the time we'd finished trudging up staircases, my hair was back to vivid pink and Jay was smiling.

Indira, blissfully oblivious, led us down a rather dark corridor and paused outside of a nondescript door. We were way at the top of the House, but on the opposite side to Milady's tower, and I'd barely set foot up there before. I couldn't say I had missed much. The walls were plain white, the passages featureless, and the windows draughty. Not so much as a curtain or a shutter was to be seen.

Indira knocked. 'Mr. Orlando, sir?'

That was extra polite, even for Indira. I felt a faint flicker of apprehension. Was Orlando a recluse because he was of monstrous personality? No, don't be absurd, Ves. Shy Indira wouldn't have survived a week if that was the case.

No answer came, and silence stretched.

Then the door opened an inch. I saw an eye peep through the crack: dark in colour, bright in expression, and penetrating. That eye took in me, Jay next to me, and Indira on her best behaviour, and then the door opened slightly farther.

'Cordelia Vesper?' said Orlando.

'Yes, sir.'

'And Jay Patel?'

'Yes, sir,' said Jay.

'Lovely.' The door swung wide, then, and the great Orlando stepped back to let us in. I smelt the enticing aroma of coffee — that would please Jay — and bread, the freshly-baked variety. Milady kept our genius well fuelled.

I have, as I said, glimpsed Orlando once or twice before, so I was prepared for his bulk. But on both occasions he had been in retreat, so I'd never seen his face. He proved to have greying dark hair cut ruthlessly short, an olive complexion, and a weathered enough visage to place him somewhere in his fifties. He wore graceless dungarees and an obviously well-loved white shirt, the sleeves rolled up to his elbows. All these characteristics clearly proclaimed the practical man, so I was surprised to note the simple bronze pendant resting in the hollow of his throat, tied on a length of leather cord. I didn't recognise the symbol.

Poor pup received a sharp check at the door. 'No,' said Orlando sternly, as she made to follow at my heels. He pointed one finger straight at her, then pointed imperiously out into the corridor.

Pup gazed up at him with adoring eyes, and wagged her tail.

'She won't do any harm—' I began, but honesty compelled me to stop right there. What kind of an idiot would turn a goldnose pup loose in a workshop like Orlando's?

Obviously I'd been planning to be exactly that kind of an idiot.

'Dear pup,' I said consolingly as I scooped her up. 'It's time to go on grand adventures in some other, less obscenely expensive part of the house.'

I hardened my heart, turfed Goodie out into the corridor, and shut the door in her face. Her doleful eyes seemed to follow me as I rejoined Jay, Orlando and Indira.

Animals are heart-rending.

'...made by a faerie king,' Jay was saying.

'For what purpose?' said Orlando, rather sharply. He spoke with a faint accent, though I couldn't place its origin. He was said to be Italian, but then he'd also been described as Polish and Croatian by various (most likely clueless) members of the Society, and on another occasion, Russian. Top marks to Orlando for mystique.

'That isn't known,' said Jay, glancing at me. 'Its present use is—'

'Yes, yes,' said Orlando, transferring his intent gaze to the lyre itself. 'I know all about its current role. But I am not convinced that is what it was originally intended to be used for.'

I'd been trying to avoid noticing the lyre, and largely failing. Orlando treated it with much less reverence than Milady and House had shown, for he'd merely stood it in the middle of a workbench set against one wall, and left it there. It looked incongruous, to say the least, surrounded by the half-finished or half-dismantled paraphernalia of Orlando's work, but nothing could hide its glorious beauty. It sat there and glimmered, its watery strings rippling, and I swear, it exuded a rosewater perfume to boot. I could smell it from the other side of the room.

'Ves,' said Jay warningly, and I averted mine eyes.

'Ah, yes,' said Orlando, and I found myself awarded the unsettling honour of his full attention. He looked at me as though he could see my inner workings, and I experienced a touch of sympathy for the artefacts that had crossed his workbenches over the years. This is how they must have felt. 'Cordelia Vesper,' said Orlando, like my name was a talisman, or a magick word. 'You are attracted to it.'

'Profoundly,' I said in despair. 'Don't ask me why. I mean, I like shiny things as much as the next person—'

'A bit more than the next person,' put in Jay, a truth which I could not deny.

'—but this is something else.'

'Describe how it makes you feel.'

I groped for the right words. 'Lustful,' was the best I came up with.

Orlando blinked.

'I don't mean like— I *mean,* it's like hunger, but much deeper. Half of me would give just about anything to take that thing up and never let go of it again.'

'And the other half?' prompted Orlando.

'The other half is scared to death of it.'

Orlando's eyes crinkled in a faint smile. 'Let us call that the sensible half.'

'And it's mesmerising. I find it hard to stop looking at it.'

'But you can manage to do so, with Jay's help.'

'He does have a way of recalling me to my senses.' It occurred to me that this was true of our friendship in many ways; the lyre was only the most obvious manifestation.

Given that I was meant to be the wise mentor here, there might be one or two things wrong with that arrangement.

Orlando said: 'It is not possible, I suppose, that Jay should embark upon this errand with some other companion?'

'What?' I said.

'Someone less at risk from the lyre's glamours.'

'Leave Ves behind?' Jay said, and I was gratified by the note of incredulity in his tone. 'No. Not an option.'

'I'm going,' I said firmly. But that said... 'When you say *at risk*, what do you mean?'

2

'I MEAN,' SAID ORLANDO, 'that this lyre possesses considerable power to bewitch, as you have experienced. But it exerts this power selectively, and I have not been able to determine why that is, or how it determines at whom to direct its glamours.'

Faerie glamour. That made more sense than it didn't. 'It had no effect on my parents, either,' I observed. 'And that's after it had chosen each of them for the throne of Ygranyllon.'

'So its interest in you is related to something else,' Orlando mused.

I shrugged. 'I haven't the least idea. Nobody else seemed to, either, among the Yllanfalen.'

'Obscurity of origin is not uncommon among ancient Great Treasures. Your mother, I understand, had some theory as to its function?'

'She's one of those who can detect traces of past magick performed in a location. She said it... amplified that ability, in some way.' Mum had been injured, drugged up and half asleep at the time, so her explanation hadn't been all that coherent. I remember the word *whoosh* featuring rather prominently.

'How?' said Orlando, with that intent look.

'I don't know. She was in no condition to explain.'

'I shall send an enquiry to Ygranyllon. For now, understand that its nature remains somewhat obscure and it must be handled with great care.'

'Yes, sir,' said Jay.

Orlando looked him up and down, as though sizing up whether or not he could be trusted with such a charge. I considered telling him that Jay was the most trustworthy person I'd ever known or could possibly imagine, and much more fitted to haul Great Treasures around than me, but a vote of confidence was clearly unnecessary. Orlando gave a satisfied nod. 'I do believe it to possess some influence over magickal residue,' he said, incomprehensibly.

'Magickal residue?' I echoed.

'Yes. But I am not sure it is the sort of influence that might be considered... desirable.'

'I don't understand.'

'I suspect it of absorbing magick.'

'*Absorbing?*'

'The way you or I might absorb, for example, a fine wine.'

'So it's a tippler.'

'Well on its way to becoming an alcoholic, I would say.' Orlando's eyes crinkled at the corners again. 'I advise keeping it separate from your Wands, or any other such artefacts.'

Jay eyed the lyre with a hard look. 'I'll keep it under control.'

The crinkles deepened. 'Doubtless. Now then, I have been instructed to share one of my newest creations with you.' His eyes brightened; if I'd imagined him reclusive due to a disinclination to share his work, I'd been wrong. 'Just a moment, please, I must find it...' Orlando set off, weaving through the multiple benches with surprising grace considering his size; he'd had practice at this dance. Every workbench was liberally strewn with objects and debris, very little of which I could put any name to. He hunted through these with such single-minded focus, he did not notice Indira at his side until she lightly touched his arm.

'It's here,' she said, and handed him the indeterminate object she had quietly picked up from a trestle table on the other side of the workshop.

I suppressed a smile as Orlando straightened up, and took the thing with alacrity. 'Wonderful girl. Thank you. Now, this is an entirely new artefact! And therefore, I hope you will not be too surprised if its form or function strikes you as unusual.'

Its form certainly did. He held the precious treasure up for us to admire, and I beheld: a glass disc. At least, it looked like glass. Something indeterminate flickered in its depths, which was interesting, but this aside there was nothing remarkable about it at all.

'What does it do?' I said.

'It... well, hm.' Orlando gave the disc to Jay. 'It is a thing of perfect chaos. There is no way at all to predict what it will do.'

'That seems...' I paused to consider what the right word might be. Weird? Unfathomable? Completely useless?

'Unusual,' Jay supplied.

'It is!' said Orlando. 'At times of difficulty, it is not always easy to determine at a moment's notice what would be best to do. No? And there is not always time to consider, either. That is where this treasure can help you. When employed, it will add a little chaos to the occasion, in just the right place.'

'The right place for what?' I said.

Orlando shrugged. 'The *right* place.'

Genius-speak was clearly beyond me.

'And I should tell you that it has not yet been fully tested,' added Orlando.

Wonderful. 'Jay?' I said. 'How about you hang onto that, too.'

Jay rolled his eyes at me, and put the panic button into his jacket pocket. 'Thank you,' he said to Orlando. 'We're very grateful.'

'I think that you will be.' Orlando looked upon both of us with vast amusement. 'Now, if that is everything, I must return to my work.'

'Almost,' I said quickly. 'I could do with some more of those sleep-spheres, if you have any.'

Orlando gave me a measuring look. I found it unsettling. 'More?' he said succinctly.

'They're handy...'

'For what?'

'For levelling inconvenient obstructions.' I held his gaze, trying *not* to look innocent, because what could possibly look more suspicious than that?

'I believe I have one or two around somewhere,' Orlando said at last, and released me from the scrutiny.

'Here.' I found Indira at my elbow, a scant three of the sleep-potion jelly-spheres in her hand. These she tipped into my palm, and I quickly transferred them to a pocket in my dress.

'Thanks.' I smiled at her, and received a brief smile in return.

And then we were outside the workshop again, ushered out by Indira, for Orlando had already turned back to his work. I cast a final glance at his broad back, bent as he was over one of his many projects, and wondered if or when I would ever meet him again.

'Odd fellow,' I murmured once the door was shut on Jay and I, and bent to pick up the pup. I'd expected her to be halfway across the mansion by the time we emerged, but she hadn't budged an inch.

'Geniuses are like that,' Jay said. I realised he was eyeing me carefully, while attempting to appear casual.

I stopped halfway down the corridor. 'All right, what is it?'

'The sleep elixir,' he began.

It was my turn to roll my eyes. 'No, I'm not using them to self-medicate.'

'Really? And how are you sleeping lately?'

'Like a baby.'

'So fitfully, and waking up screaming.'

'Jay. I'm fine.'

He took a moment to consider that, and emerged from his reflections unconvinced. 'You've had some difficult times lately,' he said, very seriously, and held my gaze with those velvety brown eyes of his. 'It wouldn't be... surprising, or shaming, if you've been unsettled.'

Part of me felt a vast indignation at such an intrusion. 'I am Ves,' I retorted, turning away again. 'I can handle this.'

The rest of me felt rather warmed by the concern, even if it had come wrapped up in a parcel of doubts. Last year I'd been sent to the infirmary for a check-up. Milady's orders. Rob had kindly but firmly questioned me on my health, my habits, and my sanity, even as he'd delivered the requisite physical examination. I'd been declared fighting fit, to my relief, but I'd seen doubt in Rob's eyes as he'd dismissed me. He'd given me strict instructions to come back the very instant I needed anything, and that had been nice.

He hadn't quite *cared*, though. Not like this.

Jay gave a tiny sigh, and I felt a pang of remorse for my ungraciousness. 'I'm fine,' I said in a more reasonable tone, and threw Jay a smile. 'Really.'

Jay saluted. 'You know best, ma'am.'

Did I? I wondered about that as we trailed down and down the stairs, clutching pup's warm little body to my chest as I thought. Is there a person alive who isn't a champion at self-deceit?

Was I fine?

'Ves,' a voice called as we reached the main hall. Valerie came floating up in her majestic velvet chair, wearing her most impish smile. 'The Baron's here. He wants to see you.'

'That's *Prince* Alban,' I corrected, swallowing down the flutter of... something that promptly threw a riot in my stomach. Apprehension? Excitement? Terror?

'I think not, when he's with you,' said Val. 'Also, there's a house.'

'A house?'

'In the driveway.'

'Great. Our ride's here.' The question of whether Alban had arrived *with* the house, and with the intention of going with us, hovered upon my lips. Considering the mischief already bound up in Val's grin, I decided not to ask.

'Then it seems we're about to ship out,' I said instead.

'The pup's going with you?'

'Yes. Actually... I need something of Miranda's.'

Val blinked. 'What?'

'I've got to find her, and no one seems to know where she is.' I brought Val up to speed, feeling secretly gratified by the angry set to her lips as I spoke. I wasn't the only one who hated her guts.

'I saw the posters,' Val said when I'd finished. 'I don't think she's here, Ves. I haven't heard a peep about it.'

Val somehow heard just about everything, so that weighed a fair bit with me. 'Right. So we're going to ask

Zareen, and if she can't help us, we might need to put this critter's nose to good use.' I hefted the pup.

'You go deal with the prince,' said Val. 'I'll get you something stinky of Miranda's.' Her tone said, *shouldn't be too hard.*

'Thanks.' I watched as Val sailed out of the hall, and took a deep breath.

Jay was staring at me again. Darkly.

'What is it now?' I sighed.

'Are you going out there?'

'To the driveway? Why wouldn't I?'

'He should stay away from you.'

I didn't need to ask who he meant by *he.* 'He's not going to hurt me.'

Jay merely raised his brows.

'Come on. Millie's waiting for you.' I turned and stepped smartly towards the door, shoulders back, chin high; *queenly posture, Ves. Zero doubts shown.*

3

THERE WAS INDEED A house in the driveway. With a supreme disregard for convenience or sense, Millie had parked herself almost directly in front of the great double-doors. I had to take a sharp left once I reached the steps, and circle around the familiar flint stone walls of the sturdy eighteenth-century farmhouse, before I saw Alban's enormous, so-shiny car.

It was purple today.

'My favourite colour,' I said as I approached the driver's seat.

His highness smiled up at me. 'I know.'

He, as always, was my favourite everything. Bright, intense green eyes, lively and full of approval as he looked at me. Bronze, artfully windswept hair. Loose, cream silk shirt.

I realised I was clutching the pup before me like a meat shield between me and him, and adjusted my grip. 'So,' I said lightly. 'You wanted to see me?'

'Always.'

At which I raised a brow, half questioning, half disapproving.

'Sorry,' he said, and reached up to stroke Goodie's soft ears. 'I'm actually playing errand boy. I've brought you some things.' He retrieved a stack of papers from the passenger seat, and handed them to me. 'That's the transcript-so-far of Torvaston's book. There's less of it than you'll want, I'm afraid. It's proving tricky to translate.'

I took it gratefully, careful not to touch his fingers. 'Thank you. I'm sure it will be useful.'

He shrugged. 'Maybe. And I've brought your new team mate. She's inside with Milady.'

So he wasn't to be our ally from Mandridore. 'Excellent,' I said brightly. 'Then we're almost ready to go.'

I waited, with the vague hope that he'd say something like *allow me to escort you to your unusually house-shaped chariot, milady,* and then never leave again.

Sadly, he merely nodded, and turned the key in the ignition. His beautiful car started up with a purr. 'Be careful out there, Ves. I'm pretty sure it will be dangerous.'

'Doubtless,' I said, with a failed attempt at a smile. 'But then, so am I.'

'Oh, always.' He released the handbrake.

'So you aren't coming with us?' I blurted. Great. So much for cool composure.

Alban looked up at me. 'I wanted to. Mother... said no.'

'And you have to do as you're told.'

He smiled, faintly. 'For the most part, yes. I do.'

What a dreary prospect. I didn't try again to detain him, and after a moment's hesitation, he said, 'Bye, Ves. Call me when you get back,' and drove slowly away.

I stood watching until the glorious Purplemobile was out of sight, for once appreciating pup's clumsy attempts to groom my face.

'All okay?' said Jay, from right behind me.

I jumped, and turned. 'How long have you been there?'

'About three seconds.'

I must've been lost in thought; I hadn't heard him approach. 'All okay,' I said, with my firm, professional, no-nonsense smile. 'We've got this.' I waved the papers at him. 'Transcript of His Majesty's Mysterious Book of Magick, or some of it. And our new associate's inside.'

Jay glanced at the empty driveway, down which Alban had just disappeared. 'Oh?'

'Yes, Alban isn't coming with us. I don't know who the lady is, yet; he didn't say.'

He was either wise or sensitive enough not to show his probable relief at Alban's lack of involvement. 'Right,' he said instead, with a nod. 'Let's go introduce ourselves.'

Our new associate was a troll with at least a dash of giant heritage, or so I was forced to conclude. We found her in the Audience Chamber — the same room, I noted in passing, where I had first met Alban. She, though, was not to be found lounging at one of the tables, supping upon chocolate and pastries and reading a book. She stood not far from the door, her regal posture emphasising her excessive height, her large hands neatly folded as she awaited our arrival. I might have expected a lady dispatched straight from the Court at Mandridore to be sumptuously garbed, but she was dressed in plain trousers, a simple shirt, and sturdy boots made for tramping about. Ready for anything, then. She was not young; her wealth of hair was snow-white, and her face wreathed in the tracery of advanced age. Nonetheless, she was unbowed, and emanated an enviable kind of vitality.

She observed our approach coolly, and subjected us both to a swift, keen look before she stepped forward to meet us.

'You must be Miss Vesper,' she said, in a low, rather deep voice. 'And Mr. Patel.'

'Yes, ma'am,' I said, on my best behaviour because — her casual attire notwithstanding — something about her self-possession and serenity suggested great power. Whether of the magickal kind or the courtly-status kind, I couldn't yet say.

'Emellana Rogan,' she said. 'I am here at Her Majesty's direction.'

My jaw dropped.

'It— I— um, wonderful to meet you,' I managed. 'Jay, Ms. Rogan is—'

'I know,' said Jay, and looked unsure whether to bow or shake her hand. He decided upon the latter, and received what appeared to be a painfully hearty handshake from the lady.

Emellana Rogan. Dear, giddy gods, the woman is the stuff of legend. She's had a thriving academic career since well, *well* before I was born; her papers and studies fill every magickal library worth its salt from Land's End to John O'Groats — and well beyond the shores of Britain, too, no doubt. She's written on every major magickal development since about 1941, unearthed a host of lost spells, dragged all manner of magickal history out of the earth with her bare hands... she's an archaeologist, charmwright and scholar all in one, and with giddy-gods-know what other talents besides.

Well, apparently one of her less well-known talents is similar to my mother's. That makes sense, doesn't it?

'I can't say that I have all your books,' I said, aware that I was gushing but unable, quite, to stop. 'There are *so* many. But I've got at least half. My favourite is *Artefacts and Alchemy,* though I also love *Charms: An Unorthodox History,* and—'

'*Bestiary of Extinct Beasts,*' Jay put in. 'Especially the part about the Wight settlements, that was brilliant—'

Jay and I were gabbling like teenagers. This realisation seemed to strike both of us at once, for we fell silent, leaving a somewhat awkward pause.

I couldn't tell if Jay was blushing, but I was. *Self-possession, Ves.* I lifted my chin.

Ms. Rogan smiled graciously, without condescension, and gave us to understand that she was greatly flattered by our immense admiration, etc.

Then she said six words which threatened to send me off into another paroxysm of awkwardness, namely: 'I enjoyed your thesis, Miss Vesper.'

She had read my thesis? *My* thesis! I couldn't speak.

'Um,' I croaked after a moment. 'Call me Ves.'

Very smooth.

But she nodded, and said: 'Call me Em.'

Unthinkable.

Jay stepped into the breach. 'So, you are a... I'm sorry, I don't know the term for what Ves's mother does.'

'It is an uncommon art,' said... Em. 'And not much regarded, its uses being considered few. As such, I am unsure a term has ever been coined for it. But yes, I am able to detect traces of past magicks performed.'

'You'd think such a talent would be more useful,' I said, interested out of my paralysis.

'It is vague,' said... Em. 'That is its primary drawback. I can determine that some manner of magick was once conducted in this hall, for instance. But what of that? There are traces of many kinds of magick done here, as well there might be. It is difficult to say for certain what kinds of magick they were; impossible to say what they were intended to achieve, when they were performed, or by whom. Therefore, it is of little relevance. I am hoping, however, that your lyre may be able to assist me there.'

'It's on its way down,' said Jay. 'Orlando thinks it absorbs magick, too.'

Emellana Rogan appeared highly interested in this nugget of possibility. 'Absorbs?' she said sharply. 'I understood it to amplify — certain things, at least.'

'Both, perhaps?' said Jay.

'And that would make some sense,' I put in. 'The lyre amplifies some arts *because* it's full of absorbed magick.'

'Which arts?' said Emellana.

'We have not yet had much opportunity to test it,' said Jay.

'Field tests are always so much more amusing,' said Emellana, with the trace of a smile, and I liked her excessively all over again. 'Are we, otherwise, ready for departure?'

'Yes, ma'am,' I said. Jay and I had been packed and ready to go for days. Our various goods and supplies would have been delivered to Millie's parlour by now, Mauf included; we awaited only Emellana, and the lyre.

I heard the click of small claws on marble as my pup came trotting in. She gave that little, triumphant *yip* that says: 'Found you!', and galloped past me in favour of acquainting herself with Emellana.

Emellana bent down at once, her face wreathed in delight. 'I'd heard of your little companion,' she said. 'To think! A goldnose, alive again in England!' She and the pup declared themselves delighted with one another, through a series of ear-rubs, belly-barings and yips. 'Are there more?' she added, looking up at me.

'No... well, not in this Britain, anymore. There are hundreds of them on the fifth.'

'I have scarcely felt a greater anticipation than when I heard of this fifth Britain,' said Emellana, her faded blue eyes alight. 'Is it as wondrous as I imagine?'

'We have seen little of it, yet, but still I'd say yes,' I answered.

'Now's our chance to see a lot more,' put in Jay.

Emellana straightened with alacrity, and smiled. 'Very well, let us not delay any longer. Can this lyre be retrieved? I shall await you in the house.'

We separated three ways: Em to Millie's parlour, Jay to enquire after the lyre, and me to find Val and the promised article of Miranda's.

I found her still in Miranda's room, or what used to be Miranda's. Was it significant that the room had not yet been reassigned? Was Milady hoping Miranda could be persuaded to come back?

If her expertise was as rare as Milady suggested, then the most likely answer to that was "yes." Good luck with that. The Society could hardly be in a hurry to welcome her Home.

'There isn't much here,' Val said as I walked in. 'I'm having trouble finding anything useful.'

I saw her point. Miranda had a suite of three rooms: a living room and kitchen, a bathroom and a bedroom. The kitchen still contained its complement of utensils and pans and such, but besides that, the place was mostly cleaned out. Miranda hadn't planned to come back; that much was clear.

I did recall, though, that Miranda often had a somewhat messy appearance. Her hair was coming out of its tail; her jumpers had holes in; she'd often forgotten something and had to go running back for it.

'Checked under the bed?' I asked.

Val just gave me a withering look from her magickal equivalent of a wheelchair.

'Right.' I crossed back to the bedroom and dropped to the floor. A few minutes' crawling about on my belly might have been dusty and undignified, but I did procure one, potentially useful item. I jumped up, waving it triumphantly.

'A stocking?' Val said. 'Really?'

'I would've much preferred an old jumper or something, too, but this'll do.' Given the quantity of dust coating the flimsy thing, I wasn't sure how much of Miranda's scent might still be discernible from it. But I trusted the pup's enormous nose.

'Rather you than me.' Val floated away towards the door. 'Call me when you get back. And be careful out there, hm?'

People kept saying that to me lately. 'Will do,' I called after her, and stuffed the stocking into my pocket. Next stop, Mellicent Makepeace.

4

'Wow, *Millie*,' I said, and whistled. 'You. Look. *Fine.*'

When Alban had promised to see Millie Makepeace — or rather, the two-hundred-year-old farmhouse she haunted — appointed a royal residence, I'd taken it as a convenient bribe. The circumstances at the time had been a trifle pressing, after all. Apparently he'd meant every word, for Millie had been *sumptuously* refitted.

I mean, her exterior walls were much improved: window frames repainted, glass and doors replaced, stonework repaired, that kind of thing. But the house was still an ordinary, modestly-sized farmhouse.

Inside was a different matter. Upon walking into her parlour, I received an eyeful of polished mahogany parquet floor strewn with plush rugs; handsomely wainscoted walls; long windows fitted with silken drapes; and an array of elegant (and to my semi-expert eye, authentic) eighteenth-century furniture. The best kind. Ornate couches, gilded and upholstered in pale blue damask. Mahogany side-tables with scrolly bronze carvings. A towering, polished cabinet bearing a vast, elaborate mirror. Etc.

The works.

'Fit for a queen,' Jay agreed, smiling at me. He sat ensconced in a pretty, curved-back chair upholstered in silvery damask, the pages of Torvaston's book open on his lap.

Am I not? agreed Millie happily. *Her Majesty herself sat in that very-same chair, Mr. Patel!*

'Clearly I've chosen the best, then,' Jay said.

Emellana Rogan sat in a matching chair on the other side of Millie's majestic, carved fireplace. It was lucky the house had been refurbished for use by the Troll Court, I thought, as the furniture was all suitably sized up to accommodate their greater proportions. Ms. Rogan would be in no way inconvenienced — and neither would the chairs.

'Any luck?' she said.

I retrieved the stocking and waved it briefly in the air. 'Best we could do. Where's pup?'

Emellana gestured at her lap, and I drifted closer. Pup was curled up there, fast asleep. So dwarfed was she in contrast to Emellana's size, I hadn't noticed her.

To my shame, I experienced a momentary stab of pure jealousy. What was Goodie doing sleeping with adorable, puppy trust all over someone who wasn't me? Or Jay?

Still, she looked happy and so did Em, so I swallowed the feeling. *Unworthy, Ves.*

'Checklist,' I announced. 'One pup with improbable gold-sniffing powers: check. One Lady of Mandridore with improbable magick-sniffing powers: check.'

'One unreasonably talkative but conveniently knowledgeable book: check,' said Jay, and I spotted the purple-clad form of Mauf lying by his chair.

'Unreasonably?' said Mauf, in a dangerous tone.

'Conveniently, wittily, superbly talkative,' Jay amended.

Mauf riffled his pages, and slammed shut his front cover with a theatrical puff of dust.

Jay suppressed a grin. 'One set of incomplete kingly notes on the sources of magick: check.' He tapped the paper in his lap.

'Wands?' I said. 'Geniusware from our favourite eccentric?'

'Double check,' said Jay.

I looked at Emellana, who nodded serenely. I looked forward to seeing what kind of a Wand *she* carried.

'Great. Fabulously expensive scroll-case etched with map of destination?'

'Check,' said Jay again. 'I've put it with Mauf.'

Not a bad idea. I wasn't sure if Mauf could absorb maps the way he could absorb text, but it wouldn't hurt to try. Just in case we were careless enough to lose a scroll-case that must be worth hundreds of thousands of pounds.

I shuddered inwardly at that thought, and swiftly reminded myself that the map was actually the valuable part.

'Dangerously beautiful moonsilver lyre?' I said.

Jay developed a guarded look. 'I've got it.'

'Where?'

'You don't need to know that right now.'

Fair enough. 'Unicorn-summoning pipes...' I began, and then frowned. 'Wait. Can I summon Adeline from a different Britain?' I was staring, for some reason, at Jay.

'How the hell should I know?' Jay said.

'Fair. Sorry. Hang on.' I left the house again, fished out my silver syrinx pipes, and blew an airy melody upon them. I mean, I'm usually a fan of the Trial and Error approach, but this was one occasion where it had to be a bad idea. What if we got there and I found Addie couldn't hear me from all the way over wherever-the-fifth-Britain was? Or couldn't reach me?

Would the absence of one unicorn make or break the mission? Probably not, but who wanted to risk it when you were working for the queen?

Not me. And Milady had specifically recommended taking Addie along.

Addie arrived on foot, this time (on hoof...?). She came trotting between two of the great, ancient oaks that line our driveway, head held high, silvery mane streaming in the wind. The balmy sunshine of early June glittered charmingly off her pale, coiled horn.

She came right up to me and shoved her face into my chest. Bump.

'Should I be calling you Ylariane?' I said, running my fingers through her silky mane. I'd recently learned that to be her true name — or at least, one of them. Apparently she was a venerable old lady; who knew how many friends she'd made, or how many names she'd been given, in all that time? Ylariane was her name among the Yllanfalen. Pretty. Ethereal. Fitting.

I couldn't get used to it.

'Addie,' I said decisively. 'I haven't got any chips for you. Let me be up front about that right now.'

Adeline snorted, most inelegantly.

'And,' I went on. 'In a minute I'm going to make you walk through a human-sized door into a perambulatory Royal Troll Residence and sit tight while we fly through the aether into Elsewhere. You okay with all that?'

My favourite unicorn sneezed on me.

'Great!' I said heartily. 'Let's go.' I took hold of a section of her mane and wandered doorwards. Addie placidly followed after — until we came to the door, which Millie invitingly opened for us. There she stopped.

'Please?' I wheedled. 'It's nice in here. Fit for a unicorn-friend-of-kings. Come on.'

Addie gave me the kind of flat stare that heralded immediate doom. I pictured myself nicely diced into bite-sized cubes, and swallowed.

'Righto. Second, then.'

I made a call. 'Val? Logistical problem here. Can you get hold of the kitchens for me?'

Ten minutes later, Addie's chips arrived. I'd pictured maybe a bowl full, but the kitchens had sent an enormous tub of them. There must've been three kilos, at least.

I stole one. Fresh, crisp and hot.

Perfect.

'Thanks,' I beamed at the obliging kitchen staff: two bright young things, both too obviously thrilled at experiencing a real unicorn sighting. They retreated a ways, and stopped.

Well, okay. I didn't really want to do this with an audience, but given the promptitude with which they'd delivered Addie's snacks, I hadn't the heart to dismiss them. Let them witness my humiliation if they must.

'Miss Adeline,' I said, backing up quickly towards the door. Addie's nose was already twitching; she'd caught the scent. 'Every single chip in this tub is yours if you follow me through that door.' I thought a moment, and in all honesty had to add: 'Almost every chip. One or two are mine.'

Addie drifted towards me, as though drawn against her will. I quickened my steps, unwilling to become the splattered victim of an out-of-control-unicorn charge, and almost fell over Millie's lintel.

Jay caught me from behind. 'Steady. If you must drop the chips, at least drop them all over the floor in here, not out there.'

'You know what? Great idea.' I tipped up the tub, letting a stream of chips fall all over the threshold. The rest I strewed all over the beautiful parquet in the short hallway beyond, and then through the parlour.

Addie, wonderful girl, dipped her head and went through the fallen chips like a lawnmower. With a brief helping hand from Jay, she was through the door and storming the hall, devouring chips at the rate of at least eight per second.

Jay slammed the door behind her. 'Go!' he called.

Where to, good ladies and gentlemen? Millie had apparently had a manners upgrade, too.

'Whitmore!' I said, abandoning the tub to Addie's predations. 'Melmidoc's Whitmore, please.'

Departing in twelve seconds, said Millie brightly.

And with a stomach-dropping *whoosh*, an unpromising rumble of stonework, and a little light chamber music, off we went.

I... AM SINKING, SAID Millie shortly afterwards.

'What?' I leapt up from my involuntary recumbent posture on the parlour floor, and dashed to the window.

Beyond it I saw the bluish-grey expanse of an English sea, and... well, that was it.

'Millie, how close to the water are we?'

I was aiming for the top of the cliff, said Millie, without quite answering my question.

'And what happened?'

I missed.

Jay joined me at the window. 'Can you jump again?'

Jump, Mr. Patel?

'You know.' Jay made up-and-over gestures. 'Travel again. Up a bit.'

I whirled about and ran down the hall. As I'd feared, water was beginning to seep under the door. 'Millie, you need to move. Now.'

I am tired! Make me stop sinking!

'We cannot, but you can. Come on, Millie.' The house was beginning to lean, slowly but surely, to one side as it sank. 'I know this is hard for you, but—'

Ohh, said Millie, cutting me off. She had gone in an instant from half-panicked whining to... purringly appreciative. *Very good, thank you.*

Bemused, I went back into the parlour. Jay was hastily scooping up Mauf and the scroll-case and moving them farther away from the windows and doors; Addie huddled against the far wall, her rump bumping the mahogany sideboard, sniffing sadly at the empty chip tub; and Emellana leaned casually against one wall, watching my unicorn with a smirk of amusement.

'Millie?' I said. 'What?'

Emellana gently patted the wall, and Millie said: *Just a little more...*

I raised an eyebrow in Emellana's general direction.

'She needed a boost,' she said, as though that explained everything.

'What did you do?'

'Supplied it.'

What had she done, applied some kind of magickal jumpstart to a... house?

Apparently, yes, for the farmhouse lurched and shifted, and with a horrible sloshing, sucking noise of loosened sand and swirling saltwater, we rocketed off the beach and upwards.

Too fast.

I clutched at the nearest sofa, waiting for a crashing sound and a sickening impact as we collided with the cliff face.

There came a crunch and a grinding noise, and the house tipped sideways, sending the lot of us sliding abruptly left.

'Millie!' I yelled as I hit the wall with a *thud.*

Sorry! She trilled.

We tipped back to the right. I collided, somehow, with Jay, and the pair of us went tumbling down.

I spared a moment's fervent prayer that Adeline wouldn't be joining us down there.

Whitmore Cliff! Millie announced, with enviable serenity.

'Thanks,' I groaned, and peeled myself off Jay. Back on my feet, I took a brief inventory of my wounds.

A few things hurt, particularly my left shoulder where I'd hit the wall. I flexed and turned; nothing was broken.

Right, then.

Jay was vertical; Emellana, too, who still held my pup in her capable hands. All appeared sound, so I turned my attention to Adeline.

'You deserve another vat of chips after this,' I told her as I coaxed her up from the floor. 'But you shan't have one, or you'll be as fat as a barrel.'

Adeline whinnied and stamped, head tossing, eyes wild.

'...I think I'd better get her out of here,' I decided, nimbly avoiding her kicking hooves.

'Post-haste,' Jay agreed.

All I had to do, as it turned out, was open the front door. Addie ran down the little hallway at a canter, and hit the grass beyond at full gallop.

I followed.

Millie had contrived to hop to about the highest point on the island; Melmidoc's shining spire towered not far away, and the treacherous sea was reduced to a distantly glittering blue-grey ribbon on the horizon.

One corner of the farmhouse was rather crushed, its newly-mended stonework crumbling. 'Lucky you've got royal patrons now, Millie,' I grumbled.

Jay emerged from the house, carrying Mauf and the scroll-case, both of which he put into my hands. The pages of Torvaston's translated book stuck out of Mauf's front cover.

I stuck them into my trusty shoulder-bag. 'The lyre?' I asked, when he made no move to go back inside.

He just winked at me.

'That... that isn't an answer.'

'I know.'

'We aren't leaving it in the house?'

'No, certainly not.'

'Then... Emellana's got it?'

He merely smiled at me.

'I dislike secrets, sir. You should know that.'

'Untrue. You *love* secrets — except when they're withheld from you.'

'Which is exactly what you're doing.'

'It's for a good cause.'

'That being?'

'Your sanity.'

I considered that. 'I concede the point,' I reluctantly said.

Emellana emerged into the cool air, still clutching the pup. She did not appear inclined to transfer Goodie into my care, and pup herself just lay there, like an inert and smiling log.

I had to scowl.

'I suppose it's all right for pup to ride with you for a bit,' I said, as graciously as I could, which wasn't very.

Emellana gave me a serene smile. 'She is very tired.'

To which, I had no particular response to offer.

5

Ashdown Castle was gone.

Believe me, I checked thoroughly. I don't know where I thought Zareen might have managed to hide a huge medieval castle-manor on an open beach, but I trawled up and down the sand anyway, twice over, before I was prepared to concede that it really wasn't there.

This was good, for it meant (hopefully) that Zareen had succeeded in finding a better, permanent home for the place. Considering its weight, it really shouldn't have been left any longer on sandy ground.

It was bad because that meant Zareen and George were nowhere within reach.

So much for our easy (maybe) link to Miranda.

We made a slightly forlorn group for a moment there, Emellana and Jay and Adeline and I, faced with the utter absence of an entire castle, and our friends with it.

Well, Jay and I did. Adeline attempted to eat a crab, and swiftly regretted it. Emellana maintained an enigmatic silence.

'I suppose Melmidoc might know something,' I offered, half-heartedly.

'Do you think Zareen was much in contact with him?' said Jay.

'Not really.' Zar wasn't the type for dutiful check-ins, especially with someone she would consider wholly uninvolved with her business, and therefore irrelevant. 'But it's somewhere to start. Even if he doesn't *know,* he can help. I mean, where would Miranda go, if she'd stayed here?'

'Wherever the rarest magickal beasts are,' said Jay promptly.

'Right. And Melmidoc would know *that,* for sure.'

'You are trying to find a colleague?' said Emellana.

I grimaced. 'Ex-colleague.'

Emellana's raised brow invited elucidation, which I provided. It made for a surprisingly brief story.

'Why do you need her?' said Emellana, gazing thoughtfully over the sea.

'We *don't,*' I said, with a ferocity that surprised even me.

Jay gave a slight cough. 'Milady insisted upon it.'

'And you always do what Milady requires.'

'Not… always,' honesty compelled me to admit. 'But mostly. And she is right about Miranda's expertise. If we find griffins or unicorns, we may be glad of her presence.' Maybe.

Emellana said nothing. Her silence proved more eloquent than any counter-argument might have been.

I watched her for a moment. Her serenity was… slightly unnerving. I mean, here we were on the mythical fifth Britain, a place even the Court at Mandridore had known nothing about until recently. A place overflowing with magick, brimming with all the lost arts and artefacts and beasts we could only dream of. *I* was itching to get off the isle of Whitmore, at last, and explore what lay on the mainland beyond the sea. Jay, I knew, was feeling the same.

Emellana Rogan, however, was… unimpressed. She stared out over the sea as though it were *just* a sea, any sea, and not teeming with magick and probably full of selkies and mermaids and naiads and… ooh, what if there *were* mermaids down there?

There could be.

'Jay! Do you think there are mermaids in those waters?' I said.

He gave me the side-eye. 'No idea. Let's pop down and check.' He started to remove his boots.

I grabbed his arm. 'Not now. Later.'

His eyes grew wide. 'You're actually serious.'

'Weren't you? Oh.' Abashed, I folded my arms, and attempted to mimic Emellana's cool, wordless stare over the water. A balmy sea-breeze blew back my hair. 'I knew that.'

Jay grinned. 'Do you want to try the stocking trick or not?'

'The wha— oh.' In the bustle and confusion of departure, I'd managed to forget about Miranda's stocking. I dragged it out of my pocket, and cast about for the pup.

She was thirty metres up the beach, snout down in the sand, digging furiously.

'Hey, she's found something,' I said, and set off after her at a trot.

Jay followed after. 'Imagine what it could be. A gold crown studded with jewels. A priceless gemstone Wand. A cache of selkie's pearls.'

'Now you're teasing me,' I said with dignity.

He laughed. 'Someday, one of your wild ideas will turn out to be true, and you'll have the last laugh.'

'Not this time,' I said mournfully, for having scooped up the pup (to her loudly-voiced dissatisfaction) I discovered her unearthed treasure to be... a coin.

I picked it up. 'They're still using shillings,' I said, showing it to Jay. It was bright and new, and obviously had not spent long buried in the sand.

'No new money? Interesting.' Jay stuck it in his pocket. 'About ten thousand more of those and we'll be rich. Good job, Goodie.'

I attempted to interest my writhing little friend in Miranda's stocking, but her response to it was to sneeze heartily, three times in quick succession. I set her down in the sand, hoping she might take off in pursuit of our missing ex-colleague, but she only sat on her haunches, ears drooping.

'To be honest, I'd probably react the same way,' said Jay.

'Her pure little heart beats only for filthy lucre,' I said with a sigh, and put the stocking away again.

Emellana joined us at a casual stroll, her large hands pushed into her coat pockets. It *was* a little nippy on the beach. 'We appear to have an imminent visitor,' she said, and pointed up the cliff.

Poised upon the edge was a familiar, pale spire, its walls twinkling faintly blue. 'I suppose it was too much to expect we could show up here without Melmidoc finding out about it,' I said.

'Especially if we park the car right next door,' said Jay.

'There is that.' The spire loomed far up there, an obvious summons. Was he coming down, or were we expected to go up?

I waited, but the spire did not move again.

'Righto, then,' I said, and trudged off in the direction of the winding path upwards. 'Let's find out what Melmidoc knows about the Vales of Wonder and the Something Mountains.'

THE SPIRE'S HEAVY DOOR swung slowly inwards as we approached, with an ominous creaking noise.

I don't know why I found this essentially inviting gesture intimidating.

'Good morning, Mr. Redclover,' I said, extra brightly to cover my unease. 'We—'

You took them all away, Melmidoc thundered, cutting me off. *Is that not what you promised?*

'What?' I blurted, taken aback. 'Who? You don't mean… Ancestria Magicka?'

The interlopers, and their inappropriately sized conveyance.

'The castle's gone now,' said Jay helpfully. 'We checked.'

And its occupants? said Melmidoc.

'Do you mean George?' I suggested. 'He stuck with Zareen, but only to get the castle moved. They should both be—'

Who in the blazes is George? thundered Melmidoc.

I suppose that answered my question as to whether Melmidoc knew what had become of Zareen.

'*Who* have you seen?' I said.

That woman.

'More specifically?' My thoughts went to Zareen first, then Miranda. Neither seemed to deserve such an epithet.

About her, *there is the arrogance of a born leader.*

Definitely not Zareen or Miranda. 'You cannot mean… Fenella Beaumont?' I said.

Emellana stiffened beside me. '*That* woman.'

My thoughts whirled. We had heard of her only once, since we'd turfed the lot of them off Whitmore. On that one occasion, she had recently made a wreck of poor Millie Makepeace.

Since then, nothing. She'd vanished. If I had given the matter much thought, I'd probably assumed she and her rotten followers were busy finding a new base of operations.

Perhaps not.

'Just when did the castle disappear?' I said around a growing feeling of foreboding.

Ten days ago, said Melmidoc. *And you have not yet answered my question.*

'I didn't hear a question, I heard a deal of shouting.'

Why are they returned? You claimed we were rid of them!

'I doubt I said anything so foolish, considering we are in no way in control of their actions.' I spoke rather absently, my mind turned upon Zareen and George and Ashdown Castle. Had they removed it, or had Fenella somehow reclaimed it? 'Where was Fenella, when you saw her? What was she doing? Who did she have with her?'

She and three souls, Melmidoc began.

'Oh, so only four of them, that isn't bad—'

Four is four too many! he snapped.

'Sorry.'

She and three souls, he said again. *Skulking about the beach at night, as though we would not know!*

'What did you do?' said Jay.

Repelled them.

I did not like the way in which he said this, suddenly cool where before he'd been ablaze with wrath. 'Um,' I put in. 'What does repelling Ancestria Magicka involve?'

They are in one of the other Britains now.

'One of them? You don't know which?'

It is immaterial.

I swallowed. 'Right. And was this before or after the castle vanished from the beach?'

After.

So it could still have been either Fenella or Zareen who was behind that little event. I was prepared to hope it was

Zareen. What was Fenella doing "skulking" around on the beach, if she'd already retrieved her castle?

I made a mental note not to get on Melmidoc's very bad side. We were on his somewhat bad side already; any more, and we'd be expelled to some other Britain in Fenella's wake. Which one was she on? Was it one that had banned all magick, or one of the ruined ones?

'We are very sorry,' I said hastily. 'We did not imagine she would find the means to return so soon.'

So soon? You knew it was likely to occur eventually?

'She's tenacious. It would take more than an ignominious banishment and a dose of amnesia to put her off.'

Perhaps a second ignominious banishment will be sufficient.

I privately thought not, supposing she managed to return from whichever Britain she was now skulking about on.

'Do you know how she got here?' said Emellana.

Madam, I believe we are unacquainted.

I sighed inwardly. Melmidoc was ever irascible.

'So we are,' said Emellana mildly. 'I am Emellana Rogan, scholar and Lady of the Court on the sixth Britain.'

'New Court,' I put in quickly. 'Not Farringale.'

Emellana raised a brow at me.

'Melmidoc has a few issues with the Old Court,' I supplied.

I *felt* him glower. *I cannot bid you welcome, madam,* said he waspishly. *You are uninvited.*

'It was quite rude of me,' Emellana agreed. 'There is some urgency about our errand.'

I rubbed at my eyes. Was that a headache coming on, already? 'Em, Melmidoc Redclover died about four centuries ago. Before that, he was one of the most visionary magickers of his age. He and his brother built this place, and pioneered the kind of advanced Waymastery that permits travel back and forth between Britains.'

Emellana made a kind of bow. 'An honour.'

Your errand? said Melmidoc. Still waspish, but, perhaps, slightly mollified.

'We seek the Vales of Wonder,' said Emellana.

There was a pause. *To what end?* said Melmidoc at length.

Emellana looked at me.

Here was the tricky part. How to tell Melmidoc that we were in pursuit of the last king of Farringale? He could hardly welcome such news. He'd spit, and snarl, and refuse to help. I'd have to handle him delicately, manage him very carefully, turn a deaf ear to his sarcastic commentary...

Ah, screw it.

'We're looking for the last king of Farringale,' I said.

6

Jay coughed. I suspicioned it might have been a strangled laugh. 'Torvaston is an interesting figure,' Jay quickly put in, before Melmidoc could blow his proverbial stack. 'He had some theories about the sources of magick, which are of considerable significance to us. His disappearance into your Britain is a mystery we'd like to solve.'

Why? demanded Melmidoc, all bluntness. *You were well rid of him.*

'Were we?'

Melmidoc made no answer.

'Because we want to restore Farringale,' I said. 'And *that* is because the decline of magick in our — and your — Britain can, debatably, be traced back to that approximate era. It's been withering away for four centuries and we'd like to stop it.'

I paused for breath, feeling peculiarly as though I'd just said something momentous. I hadn't really... had I?

Jay, though, was staring at me. 'Is that what we're really doing, Ves?'

'What?'

'Bringing magick back.'

I blinked, and thought. 'Yes,' I decided at last. 'Of course it is.'

Of course it was. It could never be enough simply to halt the decline of magick, though that would be a good place to begin. If there was the faintest chance we could reverse the trend entirely, and set it burgeoning again — why wouldn't we go after that? How could we resist?

Melmidoc was uncharacteristically quiet. 'Mel?' I said after a while.

You do not know where it will end, he said. He sounded, for some reason, subdued.

'Be careful what you wish for, etc. We know.'

I do not think you do.

'Then, tell us.'

But Melmidoc was silent.

'Show us, then,' said Emellana. 'The Court at Mandridore is committed to this goal. As their representative, I am scarcely less so. Why should we hesitate?'

Go, said Melmidoc.

I sighed, wearied with his obstreperous attitude. 'Fine.'

To the Vales of Wonder, Melmidoc continued. *Go there if you must. You will see for yourselves.*

As Torvaston had, I wondered? An excess of magick had made short work of old Farringale, that was for sure. But Torvaston would have taken those lessons away with him, when he left for the fifth Britain. He wouldn't permit such mistakes to be repeated.

Neither would we.

Jay had Torvaston's scroll-case in his hands and was staring at it, frowning deeply. 'Now that I come to think of it,' he said. 'How do we find these Vales of Wonder?'

I peeped over his shoulder. At a brief glance, which was all either of us had had opportunity for when we'd swiped it out of Farringale, it looked detailed enough. Upon closer scrutiny, though, the map proved to be hand-drawn, and inconveniently devoid of context. Or text, besides those few printed words: *The Vales of Wonder* on one half, and *the Hyndorin Mountains* on the other. These were maps *of* those two places, not *to* them.

You will find it simply enough, Waymaster, said Melmidoc. *In Scarborough there is a developed henge you may use.*

'Developed...?' said Jay.

Melmidoc offered nothing more.

'Right. Thanks, then.' Jay put away the scroll-case.

'One last thing,' I said suddenly. 'Melmidoc. You don't have any idea where Zareen and...' I stopped. He would have little idea who Zareen, George and Miranda were, and would in all likelihood care rather less. 'Are there any outsiders left on Whitmore? Anyone from our Britain?'

No, he said, with evident satisfaction.

'Well, damn and blast.'

I waited in hopes that either Jay or Emellana might have some bright suggestion to offer — or that Melmidoc might recover from his fit of the sulks and help us out. Literally, even.

You are still here?

I rolled my eyes. 'Going.'

NOT THAT I WAS sorry to be on our way out. Ever since our first visit to Whitmore, I had been itching to cross the water, and see what the rest of this hyper-magickal Britain was like. Opportunities had been consistently lacking, thanks in large part to distractions courtesy of Fenella Beaumont and her miserable crew.

Well, Melmidoc might be a grouchy old donkey but at least he'd got rid of *her.* And for all his ungraciousness, he hadn't subjected us to the same fate.

I suppose that made us, sort of, favourites. I'd take it.

'Where do we go!' I said, once fairly beyond the door of the Spire. 'Jay! Make it happen!'

He gave me a rather helpless look, then gazed out over the town. 'Well. Somewhere down on the shore there must be a crossing of some kind.'

So there must, but now that he mentioned it… had I ever noticed such a thing before? 'A ferry?' I suggested. 'A bridge?'

Jay shrugged. 'Either would be good.'

Emellana's perfect serenity gave way to a degree of puzzlement. There was even a slight frown discernible upon her agéd brow. 'The two of you *have* been here before, yes? Did I correctly understand that?'

'We have!' I said, making up in chirpiness for what I lacked in certainty.

'Multiple times,' said Jay drily. 'We were a bit distracted at those times.'

'I could fly over, and send Addie back for you,' I suggested.

'We'll consider that as a last resort,' said Jay.

'Oh, come on. Air Unicorn hasn't killed you yet.'

'There must be a more sensible way across, and we will find it,' said Jay loftily. 'After all, those story-tellers came across from the mainland last time we were here. There has to be a crossing somewhere.'

'Perhaps,' said Emellana mildly, 'it is nothing so obvious as a bridge, or a ferry.'

'Why would it be, indeed?' I said with a groan. 'Nothing else about this place is ordinary.' I set off down the sloping hill into the town, scooping up pup along the way. 'I'm going to ask someone.'

'You don't think that will sound a bit… weird?' said Jay, striding after me. 'Hey, I know we're on an island and surrounded by water we ought to have crossed in order to get here in the first place, but where's the ferry?'

I shrugged. 'What's wrong with sounding weird once in a while? Who's going to care?'

Jay growled something, but he made no further objections.

Emellana soon outstripped me, her legs being about six times as long as mine. 'There are assorted magickal means of crossing water,' she said over her shoulder. 'Some of which would not be nearly so eye-catching as a ferry terminal.'

'Such as what?' I called.

'In parts of Morocco they use a species of levitation charm. I crossed the Lukkus in '78 in a laundry tub. Uncomfortable, but effective. In Persia in '49 I was taken over a lake by a great bird — I never did discover whether it was a simorq or a rukh, but something of that nature. Then in, oh, '60, or '61, I galloped across the Danube on horseback.

How they contrived to keep the animals afloat, I don't know, but quite the marvel.' As she spoke, Emellana kept up a brisk stride down and down the hill, ever on towards the shore. We passed a number of Whitmore's citizens, few of whom were used to seeing trolls much, I concluded, from the way they stared at Emellana. Or was it the group effect of a gigantic troll, two oddly-dressed humans (by their standards) and a unicorn clattering behind that got their attention? Maybe that.

If I stopped to talk to any of them, she would soon leave us behind, so I hastened on.

'Why don't they just have a henge here?' I wondered aloud. 'That would make everything easy.'

Jay shrugged. 'It doesn't necessarily follow that, because magick is more plentiful here then Waymasters must be common as muck.'

'How disappointing.'

'Nonsense, rarity confers value.'

'Says the Waymaster.'

'Maybe I like being sought-after.'

'They only love you for your ancestral magicks.'

Jay grinned. 'Whereas you love me for my...?'

How did I answer that? I could come up with a decent list, if I thought about it for a minute.

I decided not to.

'Excellent hair,' I said instead. 'And border-ing-on-bad-boy dress sense.'

Jay casually popped the collar of his jacket. 'I knew it.'

Emellana was fading into the distance. 'Crap,' I said. 'Better run for it.'

We caught up with our Court representative on the shoreline. Pup was squeaking in protest at being so jostled about, so I set her down near Adeline.

'I believe this is it,' said Emellana.

What? I looked up and down the beach. We'd taken the cliff path downwards at a run, and I'd kept my eyes open all the way down for a sign of something promising on the horizon. Nothing.

All I saw now was unbroken sand, save for an occasional stray figure wandering upon some distant part of it, and no sign whatsoever of a way over. No ferry terminal, no bridge, no boats.

Only a wooden post, in front of which Emellana had stopped. It was an attractive post, I had to give it that much. Someone had made it out of a length of naturally twisting elm, perhaps, or walnut, and had cheerfully or-namented its knots and gnarls with embedded gems of an appealing blue colour.

'It's a post,' I said.

Emellana smiled at it, reached out a hand, and brushed a finger against the largest of the blue stones.

And promptly vanished.

'What the—' I said, turning in circles. No sign of her.

'There,' said Jay, pointing.

I saw a clear bubble rise, and drift dreamily out over the sea.

'A bubble.' I folded my arms and watched, supremely unimpressed, as it disappeared from view. 'A *bubble*.'

'I thought you'd be delighted.'

'Me?'

'I am still speaking to the woman who spent, and I believe I quote, three glorious minutes as a pancake not too long ago?'

'I was high at the time.'

'Point taken.'

'She'll pop.'

'Magick is vast and wondrous,' said Jay rather pompously.

'And?'

'So, probably she won't pop. Neither will you.'

'We'll be swept out to sea and never seen again.'

'Chicken.' Jay stooped, casually kidnapped my pup, and before I could stop him he'd touched his fingers to the eerie blue gem and turned into a bubble, too.

'Hey!' I yelled as he drifted away. 'That's my pup!'

I wasted a few seconds on pointless fuming. Low-down, dirty trick! I mentally took back about the half of the reasons I might recently have volunteered for generally approving of Jay. 'Filthy Waymasters,' I muttered.

Adeline nibbled upon my sleeve.

'You're right,' I said. 'We could just fly over, and skip the whole cast-helpless-upon-the-breeze-as-a-bubble-of-air bit altogether. But. He *called* me a chicken.'

And he wasn't actually wrong.

Furthermore, there was the matter of Emellana. One did not wish to be humbled before one's heroes.

'Meet me on the other side, Addie,' I sighed, and before I could talk myself out of it, I touched the blue stone — cool under my fingers, and curiously watery — and that was that.

'THAT,' I SAID, A short time later, 'was awesome beyond all reason.'

Jay stared at me. 'No. No, you were right before. That was *awful.*'

'What? No! I've never felt so carefree in my life.' That was the literal truth. How exactly my doubts had so entirely vanished I couldn't say, but the moment I'd transformed I'd felt like a wholly different person. I'd sailed over the blue-grey waters like a leaf on the wind, singing in my mind the whole way.

Jay looked as though he'd been dragged backwards through a hurricane. It didn't seem fair.

I couldn't tell how Emellana felt about the process. She was, as ever, serene.

'Incoming unicorn,' said Jay, and we waited while Adeline came soaring over the waves and landed with a *thump*.

I patted her nose. 'Excellent creature.'

We had ended up on another beach; Scarborough's, I hoped. Unlike Whitmore, no cliffs stood between us and the settlement. The buildings started where the beach ended, and rose in a majestic gaggle up a gentle slope. At the top, surrounded by deep green oak trees, was a castle — looking, as far as I could judge from this vantage, more intact than most such examples in our Britain.

I was beginning to sense a pattern, there.

'Time to—' I began, but Emellana was already off, striding purposefully up the beach. You'd think she was twenty-five, not one hundred and...whatever.

'It's all kinds of humbling, being around her,' I muttered.

Jay grinned. 'Call it inspiring, and let's go.'

$$7$$

IT TURNS OUT THAT the ancient isle of Whitmore is no real guide for the rest of the fifth Britain.

Whitmore has an old-fashioned air about it, to say the least. Most of its buildings are a few hundred years old, by the looks of them, and there isn't much there to remind a person that the 21st century has indeed dawned. I suppose it's because it's still very much dominated by the Redclover brothers, who collectively haven't quite left a seventeenth century that wasn't so different from our world.

The Britain beyond the shores of Whitmore is something else.

Wandering through the winding streets of Scarborough, I saw little to remind me of my own Britain save for some elements of a shared history. Here was the same, general progression from timber-framed and white-washed houses into brickwork and sash windows; here were lordly stone-built properties in granite or lime; and here and there, a move into glass and something resembling concrete was also discernible, rather to my regret.

Of cars, though, there was no sign. No buses, no train stations, no phone boxes. I searched in vain for any trace of vehicles whatsoever; there were none.

But the streets were unusually full of bubbles and floating lights.

'Ah,' said Emellana, looking keenly at a stream of them sailing in orderly fashion along the high street, a couple of feet over our heads (mine and Jay's, anyway). 'In the early nineteen-hundreds, an essay was published entitled *On Harnessing the Magickal Properties of Light and Air*, by Adelaide Amber. She was ridiculed, which now seems a shame, considering that the paper proposed just such a potential form of transport as we see here in common use.'

'Pity, too,' I said, following the passage of a passing orb of light with wistful eyes. 'How neat and clean they are.'

'And environmentally friendly,' said Jay, with a quirk of a smile.

Strange it was, to see magick in all its forms on such prominent display. Strange, and wondrous. We passed beauty parlours and pet shops, cafeterias and banks; but interspersed with these recognisable establishments were shops selling magickal curios and treasures, a patisserie advertising "Floataway Fancies" and "Never-ending Chocolate Pots", and a bookshop, its window filled with a display of spell-tomes and grimoires.

'Nope,' said Jay, literally hooking me by the collar as I attempted to swerve into the aforementioned patisserie.

'Jay. I need a never-ending chocolate pot.'

'No. You need air, water and food, and that's it.'

'Chocolate is food! Jay!'

Jay hung grimly on.

Emellana watched us with an unreadable expression, her large arms folded over her purple cotton shirt. Then, as I writhed impotently in Jay's infuriatingly secure grip, she silently entered the shop.

Three minutes later she emerged with a gilded pot the approximate size of my closed fist, an ornate lid hiding its contents. This she presented to me without a word, then strolled away up the street. 'Henge complex,' she called, pointing to a large sign adorning a nearby crossroads.

I lifted the lid of my shiny new pot, and got a strong whiff of chocolate.

'I love her,' I said.

Jay rolled his eyes. 'You'll regret it.'

'When?'

'When you've imbibed ten kilos of chocolate in two hours and start throwing up liquid cocoa.'

'But it would be the best two hours of my entire life.'

'Really?'

'Okay, not. But close...' I put the pot into my satchel. 'Guard that with your life, Mauf. If Jay tries to swipe it, bite his fingers off.'

'I regret, madam, that I am not in possession of any teeth,' said Mauf.

'I don't take issue with how you choose to ruin his day, provided that you do.'

'Understood, madam.' Mauf's tone had developed a flinty quality.

'Henge complex,' said Jay, ignoring me with perfect grace. He stood directly under the sign, which pointed to the right. 'Complex?'

'Must be the development Melmidoc mentioned?' I said.

'How do you develop a heng— never mind. We'll find out.' Jay went right.

I looked at Emellana. 'Thank you, for the pot.'

She inclined her head. 'Mr. Patel is... forgive me, but I had understood you to be his mentor?'

'Not the other way around? Well, yes, but to be honest he's got a much more developed sense of responsibility than I do.'

'A very controlled man.'

'Not controlling,' I said. 'He discourages, but I don't think he'd ever try to dictate.'

She smiled faintly. 'I said controlled, not controlling.'

Oh. Yes, Jay did have the air of a man exerting a rigid control over himself at all times. 'Makes him sensible,' I offered. 'And hard-working. And he rarely makes mistakes.'

Emellana accepted this without comment, only a flicker of her eyebrow suggesting she might find fault with some part of my argument. But she walked on without further conversation, and I fell in beside her.

'Wait,' I said, and came to a stop. 'How did you pay for the pot? We have no money.'

'No, but your nose-for-gold has been collecting quite the hoard. I've been watching her.'

I hadn't, or at least, only closely enough to make sure she didn't wander too far. In my defence, I had to watch Adeline and Jay, too; who knew what kinds of mischief those two might get up to if I didn't keep an eye on them.

'I was... distracted,' I admitted, with a sheepish grin, and gestured around at all the magickal wonder on display. 'This is the stuff of dreams.'

Emellana didn't smile. 'So it is. But dreams can all too easily turn to nightmares.'

I blinked. 'What do you mean?'

'I mean... keep a watch on your unicorn.'

Upon this point she would not elaborate, however much I pressed, so I abandoned the attempt — and looked around for Addie.

There she was — drifting after a man holding a wrapped parcel which, I strongly suspected, held a portion of fried potato.

I hastily retrieved her. 'Adeline, darling—' I began, when, to my surprise, the chip-bearer caught sight of his pursuer and cheerfully offered her a handful of potato wedges. Then he proceeded to stroke her nose, smiling.

'Yours?' he asked of me as I came up. He was barely taller than me, with pale, curling hair and a wide smile. Something about him suggested he might not be human.

'Something like that,' I said, taking hold of Adeline's silvery rope harness. He *seemed* wholly unsurprised to find a unicorn lusting after his lunch, like it was as common as being trailed by somebody's pet dog.

'What a beaut,' he said, eyeing Adeline appreciatively.

'Thank you.'

'No, I mean, *really*. You must've paid a fortune for her. She looks like royal lines.'

Royal lines? 'She isn't really mine in that sense,' I said. 'She just... goes where I go.'

'Wild?' For some reason, *that* startled him as nothing else had. 'I didn't think there were still any wild ones left. I mean, not around here.'

With which statement he offered Addie one last chip, gave a careless wave, and ambled away up the street.

I looked at Emellana, who had quietly joined us about halfway through this peculiar conversation. 'What do you make of that?'

'Think about it,' she said. 'If unicorns are as common in this Britain as horses are on our own?'

'Got it.' No more letting Addie wander off; not if she was "royal lines". 'Where's Jay?'

'He went after the henges.' Emellana gestured, and we set off in that general direction, me leading Addie carefully through the clusters of shoppers. None of them seemed much surprised to see her, either, or no more so than you might be at seeing someone leading a race-horse down the high street.

'Wait,' I said abruptly, and stopped. 'Is that—?' A familiar messy blonde ponytail had caught my eye. 'Hold Addie for me,' I said, and took off after the figure. Unless I was mistaken, there'd been a glimpse of a shabby maroon-coloured jumper too...

I caught up to where I'd seen the ponytail and found no one nearby who resembled Miranda at all. Had I imagined it? Probably.

But perhaps not.

'Listen,' I said as I rejoined Emellana and Adeline. 'If you see a woman maybe a few inches taller than me, messy dark blonde ponytail, chunky knitted jumper, late thirties or so in age, let me know?'

'Certainly,' said Emellana.

'Might conceivably be found skulking along behind us.'

Emellana's brows went up. 'Dangerous?'

'No. Or at least, not to us. She might be inclined to wander off with Addie, though.' Was I doing Miranda an injustice in saying as much? She might be a betrayer, but that didn't necessarily make her a thief.

Nonetheless.

'Human?' asked Emellana.

'As it gets.'

She nodded. 'Right.'

THE "HENGE COMPLEX" TURNED out to be at the city's highest point, not far from the castle I had admired from the shore.

Jay had found a seat upon a chunk of limestone on the edges of the grassy glade which hosted both structures, and sat watching the henges intently.

It really was a henge complex. The centrepiece was a stone circle to rival Stonehenge; in fact, it surpassed it. Tall slabs of limestone stabbed at the sky, arranged in a perfect circle. Each one had to be at least thirty feet tall.

Arrayed around this stupendous array was a series of lesser circles, all constructed from differing types of stone. The one nearest us looked like chunks of clear quartz, except I'd never previously been outdone in height by a slab of rock crystal.

'This,' said Jay without looking at us, 'is amazing.'

'Oh?' I sat down beside him. 'Tell me why.'

'For a start, I've never seen more than one henge in the same place, let alone... what, ten? Twelve?' He indicated the entire, majestic panorama with a sweep of his arm. 'Just look at that.'

'They're beautiful,' I agreed. And they really were. Clear quartz, deep grey granite laced with something green, amethyst, beryl, something sunset-coloured—

'They're more than just pretty.' Jay might have rolled his eyes, though I couldn't be sure. 'The currents here are... I've never felt anything so powerful in my life.'

8

'I CAN'T FEEL ANY of that,' I reminded him, not being a Waymaster and all.

'Right.' Jay looked at Emellana.

She shook her head. 'I have no Waymaster's arts either.'

'One of the very few things you lack, from what I hear,' he said.

She grinned at that, seemingly a rare expression with her. 'Believe me, I would have rectified that lack if I could.'

'Wouldn't we all,' I muttered.

'All right,' said Jay. 'So this is all Waymastery, all the time. I've been here for twenty minutes or so and eight people have come through in that time. Three arrived here by bubble-express; of those, one disappeared through the main henge, and two through the jade one there.' He pointed. 'Two came down on some kind of flying carpet,

I'm not even kidding, and took the one with the milky crystal stones. And the other three were coming through the other way. They all appeared together at that one that looks like lapis lazuli, and walked out of here on foot.' He paused. 'Six looked human. The other two were, I think, a spriggan and a... I don't know, but he looked a fair bit like the Yllanfalen.'

'I know!' I enthused. 'They're just openly walking about among humankind. No glamours. We passed all kinds back in the streets — trolls, brownies, even a giant. And there was this woman who — I can't be sure, but I'd almost swear she was a selkie.'

'I'm unused to walking openly through the streets of human towns,' said Emellana, with a faint smile. 'At least, not without a fair amount of pointing and shrieking.'

'Right,' said Jay. 'There's no segregation here at all.'

'No hiding,' said Emellana. 'It's refreshing.'

'I think it's wonderful,' I said fervently. 'And unicorns aren't rare at all, Jay!' I told him about our encounter with the chip-chomping gent back in town.

He nodded. 'Royal lines?'

'I don't know, but I figure they're being bred. The way horses are back home, you know.'

'For what?'

'I... don't know. Are there unicorn races?' I shrugged.

Jay pointed towards one of the henges with a jerk of his chin. 'There, look. Someone just came through.'

The someone in question could only be a giant. She came striding through a set of ethereally-pale stones, the henge looking dangerously delicate next to her towering bulk and height. It's something to see an entire giant appear out of thin air, I tell you. It's something else to watch that same giant amble through two or three of the henges, her steps shaking the earth, and then transform into a butterfly and sail airily away.

'Where the hell are we,' I said in awe.

'Ain't seen nothing yet,' said Jay with a grin. 'We haven't even got to the Vales of Wonder.'

Lawks. If these weren't wonders enough to deserve the name, what could we expect to find at the Vales?

'I'm never leaving,' I decided.

'Have to,' said Jay laconically, standing up from his rock of a seat. 'Work to do back home.'

'It cost you a lot to say that, didn't it?'

'My heart, and about half my soul.' He set off towards the rock crystal henge, and I followed with Addie. Emellana was already twenty feet away, inspecting a large, pinkish stone. Rose quartz? Morganite?

'What I can't figure out about all this is... well, everything,' he said. 'Why so many henges? What's the difference between them, other than the materials they're made from? Do they go to different places? If so, why? How does that work?'

'Do they feel different?' I took off a shoe and set my bare foot to the earth, in hopes that might help. It didn't. I felt nothing.

Jay shook his head. 'Not significantly. Maybe as to degree, though it's not as simple as the larger ones being the more powerful. The most potent one so far is actually that little spiral with the agates.'

'Potent?'

'Yeah. As in, I feel like I could take us to the moon out of that one.'

'Hold that thought for my next birthday.'

'There's nothing up there, Ves.'

'On the moon? How do you know?'

'I have it on good authority that it's a unicorn-free zone.'

Came then a flicker of maroon, out of the corner of my eye. I whirled.

Someone was disappearing behind a huge pillar of purple iolite.

'Miranda!' I shouted. '*I see you.*'

Nothing moved, and there came no reply.

I took off at a run. 'I saw you back in town,' I yelled. 'Your stealth is about as good as your loyalty— *there*. See, I knew it was you.'

Miranda stood with studied nonchalance in the shadow of the huge, gloriously purple crystal; light shone through it, casting purplish shadows across her face. She looked exactly as I remembered: messy, disorganised, intense. Same old Miranda. Only she'd grown haggard over the weeks of her absence, and while she met my gaze with a show of bravado, she couldn't hide the guilt behind her eyes. 'Hi, Ves.'

'Hi?' I sputtered. '*Hi*? What are you doing following us around?'

'Well—' she said, and stopped.

'Well?'

'Ves, you do know you can't just walk off with unicorns around here?'

'I didn't walk off with a unicorn.'

She looked over at Adeline, who was hot on Jay's heels as he came after us.

'Not a native. We brought her with us.'

That earned me a look of pure disbelief. 'You brought one of the unicorns from back home? *Here*? You do know how incredibly endangered they are on the sixth, I suppose?'

'Milady's idea,' I said quickly.

She scowled. 'Hello, Jay,' she said as he came up.

He responded only with a curt nod.

'So,' I said pleasantly. 'How can we help you, Miranda?'

'How did you find us?' Jay interrupted.

'I saw you come through from Whitmore.'

'You've been following us all morning?' I said. 'Couldn't you have just said hi?'

'Was I welcome to?' That came with a challenging look.

I sighed. 'I won't lie, I'd prefer not to talk to you. But it does happen that we were looking for you.'

She blinked. 'Looking for *me*?'

'Aye, thee. The thing is—'

Miranda was backing away. 'Look, I'm sorry about everything that happened. I really am. I'll make amends if I can, but you don't need to...'

'Oh, for goodness' sake,' I snapped. 'We aren't here to hurt you.'

'I don't know, Ves,' she said, eyeing me uncertainly. 'Last time we talked, you looked about ready to kill me. Still do.'

'Ves is a violence-free area unless severely provoked,' I said.

Jay said, 'Does abandoning the Society and betraying our movements to Ancestria Magicka count as severe provocation?' He sounded mildly interested.

I glowered, not because I wanted to kill Miranda but because I realised I didn't. Not really. She looked so damned hang-dog, with her hair falling down, her jumper unravelling at the elbows, and those shadows under her eyes. 'No,' I grouched.

Then again, when I saw pup race into view and hurl herself at Miranda like she was her best and long-lost friend, I considered revising that decision.

'Don't touch the pup,' I said warningly.

I was rewarded for my lack of generosity by two pairs of wounded eyes, fixed upon me in joint dismay.

Pup's won me over.

'Fine, fine,' I said with a wave of my hand. Since Emellana had showed up along with Goodie, I made introductions. 'Emellana's here to help us with—'

'Emellana *Rogan*?' said Miranda, staring at Em with the same kind of awe Jay and I had felt. Then she covered her eyes. 'Oh, lords. The worst possible time to meet your heroes.'

Emellana, serene in purple, merely lifted one brow a fraction of an inch. 'Why is that?'

'Because of—' she stopped, and looked an enquiry at me.

I understood the unspoken question. Yes, I had given Emellana the story of Miranda's defection from the Society. No, I didn't want to say that to Miranda just then. I ignored the question in her eyes, and said: 'Miranda's the former expert on magickal beasts with the Society. She's to join us on this assignment.'

Miranda stared. 'I am?'

'Milady's orders.'

'*Milady?*'

'None other than.'

Miranda looked from me to Jay in disbelief. 'I thought you two were no longer with the Society either.'

'Erm. Well, it's true that we're technically working for the Royal Court at Mandridore right now. They're partnered with the Society.'

Miranda's eyes grew even wider. 'What's going on here, Ves?'

'Something pretty big.'

'I see that.'

I decided not to share all the details. Miranda was still a traitor. 'We're looking for griffins,' I told her. 'Among other such creatures.'

'Such creatures?'

'Beasts of myth and legend. Oozing magick from every pore. That kind of thing.'

'We're heading for the Vales of Wonder,' said Jay. 'Soon as we figure out how.'

'And what am I for?' said Miranda.

'You probably know more about griffins than anybody else, more or less,' I said. 'Right?'

'That isn't saying much. To the best of my knowledge, you two are the only people who've seen a live one in recent memory.'

'And charmingly clueless about it we were. Are you with us or not?'

Miranda appeared uncertain, to my indignation. Honestly, how much more of an olive branch did the woman expect?

'Are you still with Ancestria Magicka?' said Jay suddenly, with a narrow look.

'Technically,' said Miranda.

'What I'm getting at is: are you here with or without their leave?'

She grinned. 'Without their knowledge, I think. I hope.' The grin faded. 'I don't want to go back home. If I go with you, that has to be clear.'

'The beasts back home need you far more than these do,' I said, frowning.

Miranda just looked at me. 'How do you know?'

Fair point.

'Right, well, if that's settled,' said Jay. 'I need to crack on with this little collection of mysteries.' He sauntered off towards the nearest henge, hands in the pockets of his jacket, face thoughtful.

Emellana held out her hand to Miranda, who took it uncertainly. There was a handshake. 'Good to have you with us,' said Emellana.

'Is it?' said Miranda softly.

Em gave an affirmative nod, and grinned. 'I've been reading your essays for years. My favourite was the one about firelight moths as familiars.'

Miranda's eyes widened. 'Well, this is surreal.'

'Miranda,' I said. 'We need some help here. Have you learned anything about this place?' I indicated the henges with a sweep of my arm.

Her eyes lit up. 'Ves, this world is amazing. *Amazing*. You know they never had aeroplanes, or cars? Never need-ed them. Everything's magick. Short-distance travel is all about the bubbles and lights — you saw that already. Long-distance journeys are taken by henge, and as far as I can figure, there's an entire world-wide infrastructure.'

'Uh huh, and how does that work?'

'Like, you don't need to be a Waymaster to use these em-powered henges, necessarily. You buy travel tokens which seem to act as ticket, passport and charm in one. Take your token, step into the right henge and away you go, and the token's used up. It's marvellous. There's a Union of Way-masters — big organisation — who set up and maintain these henge complexes, and keep them powered up.'

'Jay,' I called. 'You need to hear all this.'

Jay had already wandered out of earshot. I started after him, calling his name — and was just in time to hear him say, with something peculiarly like a giggle, 'Oops.'

And he vanished.

'Oops?' I yelled. '*Oops?*' I set off at a run towards the henge that had taken him away, a turquoise structure whose stones crackled with a kind of lightning. As I approached, the lightning faded, leaving inert stones and no sign of Jay.

9

'JAY, YOU TOTAL IDIOT!' I kicked at the nearest stone. He could've ended up anywhere. Canterbury. Edinburgh. Prague. Burundi.

He reappeared two minutes later, just as Miranda and Emellana caught up with me. 'Hah!' he said, with gusto, and vanished again.

This process was repeated twice more before he consented to pause in the centre of the turquoise henge, trembling violently and visibly out of breath.

I looked him over carefully. He had an elated look about him that seemed out of character, and his eyes were too wide. 'You okay?'

'I have *no* idea where I just went to,' he said, beaming at me. 'But it was *amazing.*'

'You're pumped up,' I said. 'Bordering upon high. Let's have a little sit down for a second, okay?' I towed him back towards his rock of a seat, but he drew his arm out of my grasp.

'No way. I need to go again.'

'Jay, do you recall how Farringale affected most of us?'

He nodded enthusiastically. 'You were all bonkers.'

'Totally intoxicated.'

I waited for the penny to drop.

And it did, after a few seconds. 'Oh,' said Jay, with a laugh, and ran a hand through his hair.

'We appear to have found your poison.'

He physically shook himself. 'It's a pretty good feeling,' he admitted.

'I can see that. But we need you sane.'

'Hey, listen to Ves, talking sense with the best of them.' He beamed at me. 'I'm proud of you.'

I found myself casting a sideways look at Emellana, whom I would not have suspect me of foolhardiness.

She smirked at me.

I coughed. 'Um, so, did you go to the same place each time?'

'The first two times, yes,' Jay said, and sat down suddenly on the grass. 'Oops. I popped up smack in the middle of the same henge, looked like bloodstone or something like that. One of many, many. Bigger henge complex than this one, at a glance.'

Miranda nodded. 'Most of them work like doors, or so I gather. Like, each henge goes to a specific designated partner henge in some other complex.'

'Right,' Jay said. 'But I could feel more potential than that, so the third time I tried to end up someplace else. And I did. Same complex, different henge. And then the fourth time I was somewhere else altogether, no idea where, except I *think* it wasn't Britain.' He looked around hungrily at all the other henges on the site, and scrambled to his feet. 'I need to try them all.'

I grabbed him by the sleeve. 'Jay. Some other time, all right? You try all of these now, you'll lose your marbles in record time.'

'You think?' Jay paused.

'We'll be scraping your sanity off the moon.'

'But,' he said.

I waited, but that was it.

'Let's stick to the task at hand, can we?' I said. 'We need to find a way through to the Vales of Wonder. You can play with the rest some other time.'

He grinned at me. 'Thanks, Mum.'

'You're welcome. So, the Vales?'

I was looking at Miranda, but she shrugged. 'I haven't heard of it.'

'Anywhere we could find, say, a map or something?'

'There's a tourist information office back in town?' she offered.

'How about a library with a computer?'

She stared at me. 'No computers here, Ves. Remember? No planes, no cars, no tech.'

I stared back. 'No internet?'

Miranda shook her head.

'What dark nightmare is this?'

She awkwardly patted my arm. 'It'll be okay.'

I gave myself a shake. 'Fine. Let's try the tourist office, or failing that there must be a library somewhere.'

Jay was drifting away. To my alarm, he was making a beeline straight for the spiralling agate structure near the centre of the henge complex. If one of the lesser ones had scrambled his wits, what would the mother of all empowered henges do to him? 'Jay,' I said, and grabbed him. 'We're going to need to get you some coffee, and a truckload of food.'

'I'm not hungry,' Jay said, but then stopped. 'Actually, no. I'm starving.'

I nodded. I'd felt the same way after my near-drowning in magick back at Farringale. 'Do they have pancakes in this Britain?' I asked Miranda. 'Please say yes. I have a never-ending chocolate pot, but I don't think that's going to cut it.'

'No idea. Let's find out.'

But when I looked around for Emellana, I didn't see her. 'Wha—' I began, and turned in a circle.

Fortunately, it isn't too hard to spot a seven-foot-and-something-tall troll woman dressed in purple. She was on the far side of the complex, communing with the foremost stone of the amethyst henge. Communing's the only possible word for it. We went after her, and found her with both hands set to the smooth stone and her eyes closed. She looked mesmerised.

'Em?' I said softly after a minute.

She didn't open her eyes. 'Can I borrow that lyre?' she asked.

Jay gave me a shifty-eyed look. 'Turn your back, Ves.'

'What? No! I can be trusted.'

He gave me a look that said, *are you kidding me?*

I sighed, and turned around. 'Unfair.' I leaned against Addie's soft flank, and watched pup gambolling happily in the sunshine. She stopped, nose to the earth, and began to dig furiously. Another nugget of loose change about to come a-cropper, no doubt.

'Why is Ves backwards?' I heard Emellana say, absently, and then came the dulcet tones of the lyre as she strummed a brief melody.

'Because she wants to meld with the lyre and must therefore avert her eyes,' said Jay.

'Meld?'

'It has a strange effect on her.'

'Hmm.' There was no more talk after that, for a while, but quite a lot more music, and I ached to turn around and watch what was happening. I knew Jay would scalp me if I did, though, and moreover he wouldn't be wrong.

'Are you finding much?' said Jay eventually.

'Not being a Waymaster any more than Ves is,' said Emellana, 'I feel very little of anything that is happening here. Until, that is, I pick up the lyre. I suppose what I am now sensing is not current activity but past, and there is a great deal of it. Very potent.'

'It's probably been an active complex for some time,' Jay agreed.

'Yes.'

I couldn't stand it anymore. 'What is it that you're trying to do?' I said. Hey, I hadn't turned around. I was still toeing the line of good sense.

'Gathering information,' said Emellana.

I was hoping for something jazzier, but all right. Emellana was the expert on world exploration. She knew what she was doing.

'Did you know your lyre absorbs magick?' she added.

I whirled around. 'Does it! Orlando said it might, but I think he wasn't sure. What is it—'

I was intercepted at this point by Jay, firmly turned about, and left facing the other way. At least this time he was nice enough to stand in front of me, so I had a face to look at while I was talking. 'Tut,' he said.

'It was only a little glimpse.' Even that was enough to make my heart ache. In Emellana's hands, the lyre had been blazing with magick and beauty. I could still feel it. 'Moonsilver and rosewater,' I added, unnecessarily.

'Wasn't it skysilver?' said Jay, folding his arms.

'I actually think skysilver is an inaccurate name. It's more moon-coloured.'

'I'll let the Yllanfalen know your thoughts.'

'It's okay, I'll just call my loving mother.' I cracked myself up with that one. When I was still laughing twenty seconds later, I had to wonder whether Jay was the only one whose senses were a trifle disordered.

Actually he looked stone-cold sane in that moment, staring at me with one brow raised.

'Sorry,' I said, and swallowed my gigglefit. 'Erm. What's she doing now?'

'Ms. Rogan has moved off to another couple of henges. Oh, she's coming back. Second.' Jay disappeared from my field of vision.

Two minutes later he said, 'Okay Ves, you can turn around again.'

I did, to find three empty-handed people and no sign of the lyre. 'Where are you keeping that thing?' I demanded.

'You are the last person I am telling.'

'Damnit.'

Emellana wore that faint smirk again, and it was definitely directed at me. 'Look,' I said. 'Give me another sixty years and I'll be every bit as imperturbable as you.'

'I do not doubt it,' she said graciously. 'Though if it helps, I do not believe the lyre's effect on you to be particularly your fault.'

'*Particularly* my fault?' I echoed. 'It's only a bit my fault?'

'Perhaps.'

I decided not to rise to that. 'What did we find out?' I said instead.

'I believe I have learned which of these henges goes the farthest,' said Emellana. 'There are clear differences in the potency of the magickal traces left behind at various sites. Though it is possible that the more potent henges lead to places of more intense magick, and the difference is unrelated to distance. The one Jay used is only of moderate power.'

'Right,' I said. 'Keeping Jay well away from the stronger ones.'

'Hey,' said Jay.

'Give me that lyre, and you can use any henge you like with my blessing. I'll even scrape you off the ceiling again afterwards.'

'There is no ceiling,' he muttered, which I took to mean he had no reasonable response to offer.

Win.

'You didn't find one conveniently marked "this way to the Vales of Wonder" I suppose?' I asked of Em.

'It's not quite that simple.'

'No,' I sighed. 'It couldn't be, could it? We need a map.'

'Or an obliging and knowledgeable passerby,' suggested she.

'I don't see why there isn't some kind of a map here already,' I said. 'Or sign posts, or... something. How do people know which henge to use?'

'That... is actually a very good point, Ves,' said Jay.

I looked at Miranda. So did everyone else.

She opened her mouth, paused, and closed it again. 'I don't know,' she said. 'I haven't used the henges myself.'

'So how do you come to know so much about how they work?'

'I asked around. I thought I might need them some-time.'

'Nobody mentioned a handy map or something? Like the tube map. Something.'

'No. Look, I'm thinking, but I don't remember anything like that. It's like... that question never came up, like no one would need to have that spelled out for them.'

'They're doing something we aren't,' I said, and stared hard at the henges as though that would help. 'Jay?'

He shook his head. 'If you can use these without being a Waymaster, then it can't be a Waymaster trick they're using.'

'Fair.'

'It's my belief,' said Emellana mildly, 'we may be looking too hard for an unusual solution.'

'Meaning?' said Jay.

'Meaning that, while many things about this Britain are indeed wondrous, not quite everything needs to be. In this instance, the fact that we have a Waymaster with us is undoubtedly an advantage, but we need not make use of your talents on this occasion if it proves inconvenient. Miranda, you spoke of travel tokens. Do you happen to know where those are sold?'

I struggled with myself. It almost hurt, to gaze at the array of magickal glory before us and interpret it as something no more miraculous than a train service; but to those who used it every day, that's all it was.

And therefore, of course there'd be a ticket office somewhere.

'Do we have money for that?' I said, considering pup doubtfully. I had endless faith in her talents, but how much discarded currency could there possibly be?

'That is a problem for later,' said Em.

A woman after my own heart.

I collared an elderly man who was making his slow way past the gates to the henge complex and pumped him for information. He may have looked at me like I was crazy or stupid or both (debatable) but he did point out the token vendor: a short, blue-painted kiosk situated about fifty feet from the gate. All right, so it was floating two feet off the floor and didn't seem to be manned by anybody, but it nonetheless couldn't more obviously be a ticket office.

And we'd walked right past it.

'Worst explorers ever,' I sighed, and started towards it.

Then stopped. 'Wait. Why is it floating?'

There came a snort from our helpful passerby. Thankfully for my dignity, he did not choose to comment on our utter ineptitude (this time), but merely raised a hand and whistled two notes.

I paid close attention to the tone, for the air thrummed in response, and the kiosk instantly sailed in our direction.

'Thanks,' I said, with a bright smile for our helpful, if taciturn, interlocutor.

He only gave me a puzzled look, and moved off.

Ah well. Can't win everyone's admiration quite all the time, or at least not if your name isn't Baron Alban.

The kiosk took its sweet time crossing the short space between us, but while slow it was jaunty. It bobbed cheerfully up to where we stood before it settled down, and a light went on inside.

Er.

'Hi?' I said. 'We need to go to the Vales of Wonder.'

Nothing happened.

'Um, can we see a list of destinations?' Jay tried.

Silence.

In fact, the thing stubbornly refused to respond to anything that we said. After a string of uninterrupted failures, we were left stymied.

'Damnit,' I said. 'Voice-operated magick isn't a thing?'

There must be a charm or something that applied here, but how to guess it? I attempted some one or two encouraging little spells, with a similar lack of effect, but as I prepared a third option my concentration was shattered by an unexpected sound: a frenzied, high-pitched barking.

'Pup?' I said, and spun.

She stood twenty feet away, paws dug into the earth, her whole body jerking as she roared her fury at... what? I could see nothing amiss. Addie was right behind me, peacefully turning her nose up at the bright green grass beneath our feet, one eye half-closed in stupefying boredom. Emellana and Miranda and Jay puzzled still over the kiosk, deep in debate about something I hadn't the leisure to listen to. And while if someone wanted to relieve us of Miranda I wouldn't have objected too much, she was kind of my responsibility, so I had to be thankful for her continued presence.

No one else was near us.

'Pup, what—' I began, and started in her direction.

Then I saw it. A small, sneaking, hatted little *person* creeping up on my Adeline.

10

'Hey!' I yelled, and launched myself in Addie's direction.

Addie had spotted him by then, too, and did her level best to take a bite out of his black, wide-brimmed hat. He jumped back, hands up in a gesture of innocence I did not at all believe.

'Sorry,' he said, with a bright, charming smile. 'I couldn't help admiring your unicorn. I've never seen such a perfect specimen.'

I narrowed my eyes, unimpressed. He hadn't just been admiring Adeline, he had most definitely been creeping up on her. And who with decent intentions called a living creature a "specimen"? 'What do you want?' I said, taking hold of Addie's silvery harness.

'Where did you get her?' said the man. Well, was he a man? He was about four feet tall, with a brownish complexion and a lean, rather haggard face. Probably not human, but whatever he might be I could not guess.

'I didn't "get" her anywhere because she isn't precisely mine,' I replied, and immediately regretted it, for his greenish eyes lit up at my final words.

'Wild? My, my! What a piece of luck for you.'

I didn't like the way he said that, nor the speculative way he looked at me.

'She's with us,' I said firmly.

Jay joined me. I couldn't have said why, but I appreciated his presence at my shoulder, especially when he drew himself up to his full height, arms folded, and stared hard at our unwelcome visitor.

It's tricky to be properly formidable when you're scarcely over five feet tall, and sporting pink hair to boot. Nice choice, Ves.

Anyway, our creepy little intruder raised his hands again and backed up a step. 'I'm just saying. That kind of luck... she'd fetch a premium price up at Vale.'

'Vale?' I said sharply. 'Do you mean the Vales of Wonder?'

He laughed. 'Nice. And this is a cute children's story, right?'

'Is it the same place?'

He shrugged. 'Probably. Are you interested or not?'

I blinked. 'Are you actually offering us some kind of partnership?'

'Why not? The price she'll fetch will split several ways, no problem.' He beamed.

Jay shifted a fraction closer, which I interpreted as a warning gesture. He needn't have worried. I could swallow my rage when I needed to. 'You offer us a partnership, having *just* tried to steal her?' I said.

He opened wide, wide eyes. 'Steal? Would I?'

'I strongly suspect so, given half a chance.'

'Well, take me up on my offer and I won't need to.'

I glanced at Emellana. Her appearance on the scene hadn't fazed the little creep, despite her being the best part of twice his height. She returned my look, with her odd quirk of a half-smile, and gave a tiny shrug of one shoulder.

I took that as concurrence. And if the great and mighty Em thought it a decent plan, well, okay then.

'We accept,' I said crisply. 'But if you so much as lay a finger on Adeline, I'll feed you to the dog.'

He looked in silence at pup. She'd ceased barking some minutes before, but continued to growl, showing all her tiny teeth. 'It would take her all year,' he said, ungenerously, but with some truth.

'Fine. I'll feed you to *him.*' I indicated Jay with a jerk of my chin.

I don't know what expression Jay was wearing just then, but it impressed our new partner rather more than the pup's minuscule rage. He subjected Jay to a long, measuring look, then nodded once and held out his hand. 'Done.' The smile came back. 'I'm Wyr.'

I shook the proffered hand, albeit warily. Jay didn't. 'Ves,' I said. 'Jay, Mir and Em.' I wasn't especially interested in handing over everyone's full names to a thief, though I don't know why I imagined it would matter. Our lives and identities were a world away.

Wyr looked quizzically from face to face. 'Forgive me for asking, but, if you weren't taking that thing up to Vale, what were you doing?'

'Ves,' hissed Miranda in my ear. 'I need to talk to you.' Since this demand came paired with a thunderous look, I didn't feel much inclined to comply.

'Later,' I muttered.

'I mean,' Wyr continued, without waiting for a reply, 'Scarborough's not really the place to be if you're looking for a big payoff.' His eyes strayed back to Addie and he added, 'At least, that's what I would've said ten minutes ago. But luck happens, yes?'

'A payoff?' echoed Jay with a frown.

'*Now*,' said Miranda, and hauled me away by the arm.

'What?' I said. 'For goodness' sake, Miranda, if you think *you* have the right to—'

'It doesn't matter what I've done,' she hissed, and I could almost feel the fury radiating off her. '*I've* never sunk so low as to sell a unicorn! *What is wrong with you?*'

I could only stare, speechless.

'Say something!' she all but shrieked.

'You've got to be kidding me,' I said. 'You don't really imagine I'm going to sell Adeline?'

'That's literally what you've just agreed to do.' She folded her maroon-knit-clad arms over her chest and glared at me.

'Right!' I said. 'And Wyr over there has just *agreed* to be totally saintly and not try to screw us over the first chance he gets. I'm sure he meant every word of that, too.'

Some of Miranda's certainty faded. 'He'll expect you to follow through. What are you going to do when you get to Vale, then?'

I didn't like that *you*, so much. After all, we were supposed to be a *we* for the (hopefully short-term) foreseeable future, and that made us a team.

Then again, I hadn't been doing a great job of treating her like a team mate, and however justified my wrath, that was hardly helpful either.

'Yeah,' I said. 'Look, this is how the Ves-plan-of-action thing works. *One* obstacle at a time. All other bridges to be crossed when we get there. Once we've reached Vale and ascertained whether or not it is the same Vales of Wonder that we're looking for, *then* we figure out how to proceed. Okay?'

'That's crazy.'

'So's borrowing trouble. There's six of us against one of Wyr, so can we stop worrying about this and get on with it?'

'Six?' Miranda repeated.

'I'm counting pup and Addie. Aren't you?'

I think that alone of everything I'd said actually mollified Miranda, for she very almost smiled. 'Fine,' she said, and stalked back to Jay, Emellana and Wyr.

Wyr was talking. 'So you just happen to have a nose-for-gold on hand and you've stumbled over a rare wild unicorn by some happenstance, but you're not thieves? Sure.'

'Thieves?!' I stuttered. 'What?'

'Travellers,' said Jay. 'Voyagers. Explorers. Take your pick, if you like, but we aren't thieves.'

Wyr shook his head in disbelief. 'Do you have any idea how many opportunities you're missing.'

'To steal other people's stuff? It's not really something I think about much,' Jay retorted.

Wyr responded with a look of frank dislike. 'You aren't going to be much fun, are you?'

'Not even a little bit.'

'Hey-ho, then,' said Wyr, adjusting his hat, and grinned. 'More loot for me. Shall we go?'

'Let's,' I agreed.

Wyr looked at us. I realised after a second that he was waiting.

'Oh, lead on,' I said, smiling.

He held out his hand. 'Token.'

'No tokens yet. We've no idea where we're going, recall?'

He didn't withdraw his hand. 'Money, then.'

'We're a bit short on that,' I admitted.

Wyr just blinked at me.

'But,' I hastened to add, 'we do have a Waymaster.'

'And?'

'So, we don't need tokens.'

'The fact that tokenless travel is against the law makes no never-mind to you, but you're *not* thieves.' Wyr smirked.

'It... is?' I said uncertainly.

'There's a tax on... where the blazes are you lot *from?* How can you not know this?'

'We're from overseas,' I said smoothly. Well, it was technically true.

'Uh huh.' Wyr went to the kiosk, which waited patiently beside us, and acquired a token within approximately four and a half seconds. To my annoyance, I couldn't tell what he'd done to accomplish that.

He saw me watching, though, and waved the token at me: a small object that shone. 'Some of us are law-abiding citizens.'

'I'm sure.'

He grinned, and walked off towards the henges, whistling. 'Come along, then, children. We want the amber henge, first.'

First? I hoped we wouldn't have too many henges to travel between. Poor Jay would be jelly by the time we made it to Vale.

Miranda took charge of Addie, which might have worried me if it were any creature but my unicorn. Adeline could take care of herself, if necessary; I didn't give much for Wyr's chances had he got much nearer to her.

But Emellana fell in beside me, and spoke in a low tone. 'That person,' she said, nodding her head at Wyr some little way ahead, 'used some kind of a charm back there, on Adeline. Potent, too. The air is still thrumming with it.'

'*Oh*,' I said, and looked swiftly at Addie. Was she her normal self? 'What kind of a charm was it?'

'Nothing I have ever encountered before.'

'Hardly surprising,' I offered. 'Everything here is so different.'

She nodded. 'I do not criticise your decision to bargain with that one, but I do urge you to be wary. He has powerful arts at his disposal, and I cannot guess at his intentions.'

I'd been privately wondering something similar. 'If he's a thief he's an inept one,' I agreed. 'Spotted before he got within three feet of his target.'

'He may not have anticipated the loyalty or alertness of your pup.'

I drifted in Jay's direction. 'Keep that lyre out of sight,' I whispered.

'You think?'

I rolled my eyes. 'Fine. Sorry.' But I couldn't resist adding, 'And the scroll-case, too.' It was, after all, crusted with jewels worth a fortune.

'Got it, Ves. Stop.'

I gave him a tiny salute. 'Yessir.'

Wyr did not deign to wait for us. He walked straight into the circle of amber and disappeared in a shower of light.

'Helpful,' muttered Jay.

In Wyr's defence, he probably had no way of knowing that Jay could access multiple locations from these henges. 'One of the routes is probably more... well-travelled,' I suggested. Like a well-beaten track, but the magickal equivalent... could Jay tell? Why was I trying to help when I had no idea what I was talking about?

I shut up.

Jay said nothing for a while, but stood with closed eyes, one hand laid atop the nearest stone.

His eyes opened.

'Em and Miranda first,' he said. 'Please. Ves, hang onto Adeline and pup. I'll be coming back for you in a moment.'

I waited while Jay took hold of our two companions and stepped into the henge. All three of them vanished from sight.

By the time Jay reappeared, I had pup tucked under one arm, my other hand clutching Addie's rope.

'Ready to go?' he said. His eyes were a bit wild again, but otherwise he looked — so far — normal.

'All set,' I said.

He held out his hands for pup, and then took my hand. 'Listen,' he said. 'I've never taken a unicorn through the Ways before. If she comes out with her head on backwards or something—'

'I will never let you hear the end of it,' I promised.

'That's what I thought.'

We stepped between the stones, and when my feet hit the centre of the amber circle, the Winds rushed up to claim us and we were gone.

11

In the end, we passed through five henge complexes. Jay, of course, went through each set twice in order to ferry the lot of us across. By the time Wyr stopped and said, 'Well, here we are,' Jay was reduced to a legless mess.

I gathered this from his recumbent posture upon the floor, limbs akimbo, his face bathed in sweat. He was breathing far too fast, and — to my mingled amusement and concern — laughing.

Wyr stood over him with his hands in the pockets of his long coat, and slowly shook his head. 'So many reasons to use tokens like a normal person.'

'I'm using the Ways like a normal person,' said Jay, laughing, and then he began to cough.

'Oops.' I ran to help him sit up. 'Jay, we're going to take a little break right here. All right?'

'I'm fine.' He beamed sunnily up at me, and sagged in my arms like a sack of potatoes.

I let him slither back to the ground.

'Well.' I looked around. 'Let's use this time for a little reconnaissance, hm? Is this... Vale?'

I said it doubtfully, because to my admittedly inexperienced eye, there wasn't much about the place to suggest that we had arrived anywhere significant. We had emerged at a small complex comprising only three henges, none of them large. The trio of stone circles sat atop a grassy hill in the midst of a rolling, airy plain. In one direction I could see, distantly, the edge of an evergreen forest; everywhere else was simply more grass. A desultory drizzle of rain fell from a grey sky.

'Vale's that way.' Wyr pointed out at some of the grass.

'It's a ways off, by the looks of it,' I said.

'They gave up trying to put a henge complex in there,' said Wyr. 'Never worked.'

'Why not?'

'Because it's... well, you'll see.' Wyr set off down the hill, hands in his pockets, whistling a jaunty tune.

I made to follow him.

And stopped, because down there in the grass, over towards the forest, I saw a string of what looked like wild horses racing by. They weren't, of course. Even from this distance, I could see the far-off glint of the graceful horn each bore upon their forehead.

Adeline had stopped, too, and stood staring in their direction, her head high.

'Unicorns,' I said.

Miranda breathed something unintelligible but no doubt awed, and started down the hill at once.

'No, wait!' I said, cursing myself for an idiot. 'Mir, hang on a second. We shouldn't just blindly follow Wyr. Em, will you take care of Jay and pup for a bit while I check things out?' *And keep an eye on Miranda*, I wanted to add, but didn't.

Emellana nodded. 'I think it wise.'

Jay had stopped laughing or coughing. He lay silent, ostensibly dazed, though his eyes opened at my words and he looked intently at me. 'I should go with you,' he said.

'Nope.'

'But—'

'If you can prove you can stand up straight for more than twenty seconds, then you can come with me.'

It took Jay about ten to demonstrate his total incapacity for vertical posture.

'I'll be back soon,' I promised.

'I'm coming with you,' said Miranda.

'What?' I said, idiotically.

She did not deign to repeat what she'd said, but instead strode towards Adeline, one hand outstretched. Addie, the traitor, permitted herself to be petted, and when Miranda swung herself up onto her back, she made no objection.

I knew Addie could carry two passengers at once; she'd done it before. I was left, then, to fume impotently, having no reasonable grounds upon which to object to Miranda's company.

Ah, screw reasonable. 'The fact is, Mir, I don't trust you,' I said.

She thought about that. 'I can understand why you wouldn't,' she said. 'Nonetheless.' She sat there atop Addie's back, unmoved.

I folded my arms, equally unmoved.

'I swear you will come to no harm at my hands?' Miranda tried, and gave me a Brownie's Honour salute with her right hand.

'Why are you so determined to come along?'

'Because,' said Miranda, with exaggerated patience, 'if Vale proves to be as awash with griffins as you imagine, you might need me. Isn't that why Milady wanted me along?'

'Not untrue,' I conceded.

'And because I left for Ancestria Magicka in the first place because they promised me *significantly enhanced access to magickal beasts of all species, both extant and extinct,* and to be honest this is the first real chance I've had at anything of the kind. I'm not sitting up here waiting while you have all the fun.'

'Ancestria Magicka lie, what a shocker,' I muttered, but I stopped arguing. 'You're sitting behind,' I said, in a no-nonsense tone, and joined her atop Addie's back. 'Right. Em, we'll come straight back as soon as we know it's safe. If our creepy little thief comes back... truss him up or something.'

'The thief is at the bottom of the hill,' said Emellana.

'Fine. He can stay there. Hup.' I gave Addie the signal to fly, and she extended her beautiful wings as she took off at a trot, and then a canter. I urged her in the same approximate direction Wyr had been heading in, and soon we were airborne, a strong wind blowing drizzle into our faces.

I saw Wyr as we rose into the air, watching our upward progress with an expression of mild chagrin. Did he think we were running out on our deal? I hoped he wouldn't give Jay a hard time over it, but if he did, Emellana could handle him.

We flew for perhaps five minutes, over uninterrupted grassy hills. Then, I caught a glimpse of a cluster of buildings upon the horizon, and my heart quickened with excitement. 'There it is!' I shouted, and pointed.

'I see it,' yelled Miranda in my ear.

The town quickly grew in our vision as we raced towards it, soon proving to be quite large. Surprisingly so. Why should I be surprised? Perhaps because Torvaston's hand-drawn map on the back of his scroll-case hadn't suggested anything of the kind. But, it was four hundred years old. The town of Vale spread out before us, composed of an expanse of mostly low-rise buildings. There seemed to be a trend for blue paint, for some reason, for the town was predominantly cerulean and periwinkle, with white ornaments. The grey-blue waters of a wide river snaked through the settlement, glinting in lacklustre fashion in the muted light, and a network of smaller waterways wound their way through the streets.

But our attention was soon distracted from this sight, however agreeable, for right in the middle of the town rose a hill so tall it could almost be classified as a mountain. We'd seen nothing of it from a distance, which argued for its enjoying some kind of magickal camouflage; only once we were almost on top of it did it abruptly loom out of the misty skies. Its sides were unusually smooth, and thickly clad in velvety greenery. It was liberally veined with gemstones, or so I judged from the periodic flashes of colour and reflected light that caught my eye as we flew nearer.

'Look,' said Miranda. '*Look!*'

Her arm stretched past my nose, pointing up and up. I looked.

And could almost have imagined myself back at Farringale, for whirling with majestic grace around the summit of that hill was a trio of griffins. They were high up, so high as to appear minuscule. But there was no mistaking the crackle of magickal lightning that wreathed their powerful wings.

I fumbled for the scroll-case, and pulled it open. There, in fading ink, was a shaky network of rivers generally matching those I saw before me, and a shape that could reasonably indicate the hill.

'Rivers,' I said. 'Mountain. Griffins. Right.' I put the case away again, and permitted myself one more long, greedy stare at those griffins far above. There were five by then — no, six — and they were coming down. 'I think we're in the right place,' I said to Miranda.

'Unicorn,' she said.

'What?'

'Look to your left, and down.'

She was right. Way down there, just taking to the skies, was a winged horse as ethereal and lovely as my Adeline. Well, almost. Addie is, after all, the best.

'Right,' I said. 'Let's fetch the others.'

Unfortunately for us, we arrived back at the hilltop henges to find that the others were no longer there.

I stood in the centre of the three stone circles, turning about in the futile hope that I'd catch sight of Jay somewhere on the horizon. Or Emellana, eighteen feet tall and dressed in purple.

Nope.

'For heaven's sake,' I muttered. 'Not *again*.'

12

'Again?' echoed Miranda, as a brisk wind tore yet more of her flyaway blonde hair out of its ponytail.

'Jay has a bad habit of disappearing.'

'Also for turning up again, yes?'

'It's more that I have a decent track record for tracking him down. There was that time when he was hauled off by your charming new employers, because apparently kidnapping is a valid headhunting technique. And that time Millie swallowed him up and spat him out on Whitmore. This time... Jay could have gone through any of these henges, and taken Emellana with him. But why would he? And besides, he was exhausted. I don't know if he was capable of another jaunt through the Ways yet. So, it has to be Wyr's doing.' I set off down the hill, leading Addie, until I arrived at the approximate spot in which I had last caught sight of our shifty guide.

I found bottle-green grass riddled with rabbit burrows — or, *something* burrows. Did they have anything so mundane as a rabbit in these parts? That was it, really. A daisy or two made its presence known, smiling cheerily at me from among flourishing tufts, and the long slope of the hill rose behind me, discouragingly featureless.

'Here,' called Miranda, from some distance away.

I turned, and sloped off after her. She had wandered off around the other side, which made little sense to me since no one had been going that way.

But she had found something. A jutting piece of cloudy stone erupted from the grass, tucked right into the base of the hillside. At its top, a large jewel was inset. This one was green, not blue, but the general arrangement looked familiar enough.

'Probably goes into Vale,' Miranda suggested.

I realised that she was waiting for my approval before she tried it.

'Surely they'd wait for us,' I said doubtfully.

'Not if they had a reason to hurry.'

Like Jay in a state of collapse and in urgent need of food. I looked at Addie. 'Can we take a unicorn through that way?'

Miranda shrugged. 'Try it.'

I tried it. Taking hold of Addie's neck with one hand, I touched the green jewel with the other.

The world tipped and spun around me, and away I went, soaring over the deep green grass in bubble form. Probably. It isn't easy to tell in that state.

But soon enough a second bubble came swishing up beside me, which sort of answered my question, although was this Adeline or Miranda? I couldn't tell. I had only to wait, while I hurtled at insane speed over hill and dale, my stomach (did I still have a stomach?) turning itself inside out as we bobbed and spun in the wind.

Something changed. The bubble beside me sprouted wings, and antennae, and legs, becoming (in short) a butterfly. Its hue altered gradually from bluish to purplish and then it was a winged lemon with overlarge eyes and a tuft upon its head, sailing through the air just as though it had every right to fly.

After that it became a hedgehog, a cigar, and what looked to me like a cheese sandwich in quick succession.

'Oof,' I said soon afterwards, finding myself deposited with unceremonious abruptness upon a disappointingly solid floor.

I performed a brief check of my four limbs to ascertain that they were a) present, and b) suitably proportioned. They were.

'Was it my imagination,' I said to Miranda, who'd appeared beside me, 'or was I not entirely bubble-shaped for some of that?'

'You were a red cabbage first,' said she, stretching, her eyes rather wild. 'Then a purple potion bottle, and a dragonfly, and a golden flaming arrow.'

'How imaginative of me,' I murmured, looking around. 'I'm getting the feeling this is going to be an... interesting stay... Jay!'

He sat three feet behind me, his back against the brick wall of some kind of shop, judging from the sign that hung from its eaves, though I couldn't decipher the symbols that were painted upon it. We had fetched up in a town square, albeit an unusually circular one, and all around us were stone or brick-built shops with tall, tapering roofs and inconsistently sized windows. As I watched, the blue-slate roof of a nearby structure leisurely grew two or three feet taller, as though stretching itself, and then settled back down.

Jay was in one piece, which was nice. 'Have you... shrunk?' I said.

He gestured at himself with his free hand. The other held something breadish that oozed cheese, and he spoke with his mouth full of the stuff. 'What do you think.'

He was three feet tall.

'I may get to like being the taller of us, for a change,' said I.

'Wait till you see yourself.'

'…Have you shrunk, or have I grown?!'

'It's more your hair.'

I checked it. 'I have grass growing from my head,' I said, in a very calm voice.

'I'd classify it more nearly as hay, but yes.'

I took a deep, deep breath. 'Right. Priorities. Where's Adeline.'

As I spoke, a tiny unicorn zipped past my nose. Her pale coat and silvery rope harness looked familiar.

I captured her in my two hands, and sighed. 'Emellana?'

'She and Wyr went shopping.'

'Wyr! I thought he had made off with you.'

'Sorry,' said Jay. 'We—'

Wyr's dusty voice interrupted. 'You thought what? I am outraged.'

'Sure you are.' I watched him narrowly as he skulked into view, expecting to see some sign of alterations in him. There were none.

'How are you unscathed,' muttered Miranda, echoing my own thoughts. Her ratty old jumper had found a new lease of life as a gown, which would have pleased *me* immensely, especially since it was made of fiery autumn leaves and what looked like velvet. Or clouds. I couldn't altogether say. Though, I couldn't blame her for being displeased about her nose, which now more nearly resembled a beak.

Perhaps she hadn't noticed.

'You get used to it,' said Wyr. 'Your first dose of pure, prime-grade magick tends to have side effects.' He saluted me. 'Don't mind the bees,' he said. 'They'll leave you alone when your hair changes again.'

So that was the buzzing sound I'd been half aware of. I put up a hand to check my haystack, and found it merrily sprouting flowers.

'I dread to ask,' I said, letting this pass. 'What's become of my pup?'

Wyr pointed at a sparkly, polychromatic brick that lay in the middle of the square. As I watched, all the cobblestones around it pulsed, washing over with shifting colours.

'She's a brick,' I said, keeping it together somehow. I don't deny that I was beginning to feel just a touch... high.

'For now. She was an alikat ten minutes ago, if an unusually small specimen. In a minute she'll be a balloon, perhaps, or herself again.' He wandered over, and put a glass bottle into my hand. It felt positively chilly to the touch, a quantity of amber-coloured liquid sloshing about inside it. 'Drink that,' he instructed.

I must have looked doubtful; I certainly felt it. He gave me a wounded look. 'What, don't you trust me?'

I watched in fascination as his wide-angled hat slowly sprouted an exquisite, miniature lily. 'No,' I said bluntly, as the world swam before my eyes.

He grinned. 'It has your troll friend's approval, if that helps. It's a… let's call it a dampener. It will moderate the effects of Vale, at least for a little while.'

The hat grew a tiny dragon, which swallowed the lily, and then disintegrated in a puff of red dust.

'Uh huh,' I said, dazed. A giggle escaped.

Opening the bottle, I quaffed the contents.

Emellana herself reappeared moments later. She, to my confusion, looked but little affected by the chaos; even less so than Wyr, considering his bizarre hatly antics. She saw the question in my face, for she winked at me, and briefly mimed a strumming motion.

The lyre! Did she still have it? If it absorbed magick, according to Orlando's theory, then perhaps it was acting as an effective dampener by itself.

I wondered what configuration that much "prime-grade" magick might leave the instrument in. What might a magick-drunk lyre look like?

Anything, I supposed. Anything at all.

'I hope we did not unduly inconvenience you,' said Emellana. 'Jay was in urgent need of sustenance.'

Considering Emellana's unshakeably laid-back nature, when she said "urgent" I judged she truly meant it. 'Thanks for feeding him,' I said.

She smiled. 'Wayfinding can be hungry work, and I fancy the effects in these parts are more profound.' She surveyed Jay critically. 'His fourth sandwich,' she added. 'He will be able to stand again after one or two more.'

'How did you get him here if he couldn't walk?'

Emellana's response consisted primarily of an amused look. 'How do you think?'

I remembered her height, bulk and general attitude of implacable competence, and promptly withdrew the question.

'So,' I said, checking my hair. Still hay. 'What do you mean by prime-grade magick?' I addressed this question to Wyr, who was still ambling about with a sackful of goodies.

Wyr handed a bottle of green liquid to Jay. It was supremely weird to see those two about the same height. 'Lectures cost extra.'

'I will kick you for free,' I offered.

He scowled at me. 'Why did you want to come here if you don't know anything about Vale?'

'To learn about Vale,' I said.

'Obviously,' Jay added.

Wyr declined to follow Miranda to the other side of the square, and merely lobbed a bottle of something-blue at her instead. Thankfully, she caught it. 'It's a place of cultivated magick,' he said. 'Said to be the purest and most potent, hence grade-A.'

'Why's it so quiet?' said Jay, glancing meaningfully at the empty square.

'Considering the state of yourself,' said Wyr, 'Do you really need to ask.'

Jay's smile was crooked. 'Fair point.'

'Most people can't cope with it, or they choose not to. It's not for the masses.'

'Then who is it for?' I asked.

Wyr shrugged. 'It's more of a... supplier. Most of the best magickal produce is made and packaged and shipped from here.'

'And beasts?' put in Miranda. 'You implied there's a buyer for unicorns here.'

'Yup,' said Wyr.

His sudden laconic fit made me suspicious. 'What kind of buyer?'

'Why don't we deal with that now?' said Wyr, his charming smile back in place. 'Then I can get out of your hair.'

'Absolutely,' I said.

'Great.'

'But first I'm going to need to know more about the history of Vale.'

He stared at me in disbelief. 'What do you think I am, a history professor?'

'There must be a library, hereabouts?' I suggested.

'No.'

'Local history society?'

'No.'

'Venerable crone of great wisdom, dispensing nuggets of magickal lore for a fee?'

'Not exactly.'

'Internet café?'

He blinked. 'What?'

'Never mind.' Being out of ideas, I looked Emellana's way. 'It's Torvaston. How do we find out if he was here?'

Wyr rubbed at his eyes. 'Who the blazes is Torvaston.'

'Um. You might know him as…' I'd forgotten the name.

'Furgidan the Dispossessed,' Jay supplied.

'That's it!'

Emellana said, 'A great troll king, said to have settled in what were *once* called the Vales of Wonder.'

'And according to the storytellers of Whitmore,' I added, 'he just might possibly still be alive somewhere.'

'In a manner of speaking,' said Jay. 'Might be a bit ghostish around the edges.'

Wyr cleared his throat. 'The lot of you are insane, but you probably know that, don't you?'

My heart sank. 'So you don't know anything about Furgidan?'

'It's a known name in some circles.'

'Ah!'

'But if you thought you were going to pop up here and have a nice chat with him, I'll have to disappoint you. He died hundreds of years ago.'

'Ghost?' I said hopefully. I felt a touch of something warm against my leg, and looked down to find pup (thankfully hound-shaped) nosing at my shin.

'Like I said,' Wyr answered. 'Insane.'

'Fine, forget the ghost.' My pup had something in her mouth. I bent down to wrestle it off her. It was a stick... probably.

'What's known about him?' said Jay.

'Not much.' Wyr shrugged. 'Claimed to be some kind of a king, went off to found a new kingdom with a bunch of cronies... the details escape me. Why are we caring about him when we've a unicorn to dispose of?' He looked around. 'Or we... did.'

I'd been obliged to let go of Addie some minutes earlier, when she'd developed something spiky which stung my hands. Where (and what) she was right now was beyond my knowledge, but I was not unduly worried. With Wyr on the lookout, she was probably safer as a mayfly or a waterlily than a standard-issue-sized unicorn. And I could always fall back on the pipes.

'She'll turn up,' I said, and smiled. 'Listen, what if we had something of Furgidan's? Do you think we could find out what became of him?'

'What, his handkerchief or his chamber pot?' Wyr smirked. 'Don't be absurd.'

I was beginning to get tired of the thief.

'That's a lie,' said Emellana calmly. 'Isn't it?'

Wyr gave her a bland stare. 'I guarantee, Furgidan the Dispossessed's chamber pot will get you nowhere.'

'But something more personal might,' said Em. 'Mightn't it?'

'Like a scroll-case,' I said. 'With a map on it, drawn by his own hand.'

'The unicorn trader's this way.' Wyr jerked his thumb in the direction of a narrow, crooked street that meandered away to my left.

'Ves,' said Miranda suddenly. Her tone held a note of some urgency, and I looked sharply at her. She hadn't spoken for some minutes.

'Yes?'

'Those griffins.' She pointed in the direction of the tall hill we had glimpsed an hour or two before, on Addie's back. I followed her gaze, shading my eyes against the strong sun. 'They're behaving oddly.'

'How do you mean?'

'They're... their flight's too regular. It's as though they are following some kind of circuit.'

'That isn't normal?'

She hesitated. 'I haven't had much chance to study live griffins, understand. But it doesn't look right.'

Vague, but I'd take it. Milady was right about Miranda: few people were more to be relied upon when it came to magickal beasts. If she had a hunch... 'What might be causing that?' I asked.

'I don't know, but I want to find out.'

13

'How about unicorn trader, *then* griffins?' growled Wyr.

'Sorry,' I said briefly. 'No unicorn, no unicorn trader.' Not that I wouldn't have been happy to get rid of Wyr and his attitude, but he was useful. Sometimes.

And I wasn't yet sure how to dispense with him without compromising Addie.

Wyr grumbled something incoherent, and jammed his hat further down on his head. 'You've some nerve,' he informed me.

'What are you going to do, steal my shoes?'

'How about that scroll-case you mentioned?'

'Oh?' I considered his carefully bland face. 'Valuable, is it?' I hadn't mentioned the jewels. Only the fact that it was defaced by a map — drawn by Furgidan.

Wyr opened his mouth, and shut it again with a snap. 'You I dislike,' he said.

I ignored him. Jay had found his feet, and his regular height to boot. To my relief, he was looking somewhat recovered from his Wayfinding marathon, and less grey about the face. Hopefully he could tank five or six sandwiches without throwing up, but I kept a little distance between us just in case. 'The, uh, object in Emellana's possession might be of use,' he said obliquely. 'With the scroll.'

I nodded. I'd drawn the same conclusion from Emellana's words. Could she find traces of Torvaston, with the use of a magick-drenched lyre, her talent for tracking old magick, and the scroll-case to help her? I hoped so.

But first, the griffins.

FINDING GRIFFIN HEIGHTS PROVED to be a lot easier than it had in Old Farringale, to my relief. This particular hill had no interest in playing coy, or concealing itself, at least not from a near distance; it loomed over Vale, suitably solid and stationary, and we slogged through the crooked streets of the town in pursuit. There really weren't many people living there, I judged; Wyr was right. Few of the properties we passed had a residential air about them. Many were clearly commercial properties, with at least a minimal shopfront opening onto the street, and work-shops or warehouses behind.

The streets had a way of moving about. They were not doing so either for our benefit or for our inconvenience, I thought, but rather according to some purpose of their own. Roads bulged under our feet, forming slopes and little hillocks, only to dip again farther along, dropping us down and down into impromptu valleys. Sometimes they writhed like snakes before us and reconfigured themselves, curving to this side or the other of a house, and racing around corners.

One imaginative street rerouted itself right through the middle of a tall, green-painted house — with the house's assistance, I might add, for an arched walkway blossomed around us, complete with stocky pillars.

'How does anybody find anything around here,' I said after a while, when the street we were following took a sud-den, gleeful curve and apparently doubled back on itself.

Wyr gave a low, rather smug chuckle. 'You'll see,' he said, in a tone I did not at all like.

Emellana drew nearer to me. 'I believe there's mischief afoot,' she said softly.

'Undoubtedly, with that one,' I sighed, regretting my decision of half an hour before. Was Wyr useful, or a liability? 'That hill really isn't getting any closer, is it?'

'No.'

'It's not getting farther away, maybe?' I said, thinking again of Farringale.

'No.'

Miranda was so busy studying the distant griffins' flight patterns, I doubted whether she had noticed our navigational difficulties. Jay, though, had developed that dark frown of his, the one that means someone's in trouble.

After a couple more minutes, he stopped in the middle of a prettily dappled cobblestone street and said: 'Wyr.'

'Yes, sir.'

'Where are we going?'

Wyr thought about that. 'Wherever Vale wants to take you,' he answered, which sounded to have more truth in it than I'd expected.

'And is that more or less where *we* want to go?' asked Jay.

'You find that out when you get there.'

Jay looked around. To our left rose a leggy cottage with a towering brown roof and great windows like eyes in its front. To our right stood a more compact building made from blue bricks, with a sign up front reading "R. B. Wimberley, Charmwright."

'This isn't it,' said Jay.

'Then I'd suggest you keep walking,' said Wyr.

What could we do but comply? Though it did not in-convenience us for very much longer, for after another three minutes of discontented trudging, the town melted away around us, leaving open meadow in its wake. Neatly fenced meadow, to be specific, and each enclosure was crowded with unicorns.

'Oh, look,' said Wyr, with a smile of pure malice. 'The unicorn traders.'

'And how did you achieve that?' said Emellana, stone-faced.

'Didn't you hear me?' he said, beaming. 'This town has a mind of its own.'

'But it can be influenced, no? Or is that not what you were doing?'

Wyr's smile faded. 'How is it that you—'

'Newcomers we may be, but we are not wholly without arts. I am sometimes aware of the traces magick leaves behind, and yours has been leaving a fresh trail for the past half-hour.'

'Well then, you figure it out,' said Wyr. 'In the meantime, I'll thank you to produce that unicorn, please.'

'There is no knowing where she's got to,' I said blandly.

'Find her, then.' He pulled something long and twin-kling from a pocket and began to juggle with it.

I recognised the jewel-encrusted shapes of Torvaston's scroll-case.

'I *knew* you were a thief!' I said.

Wyr added a second object into his juggling, which to my horror proved to be my Sunstone Wand. 'Didn't do much about it, did you? That's the problem with you soft-hearted types. Too trusting by half.' To top it all off, Orlando's prized new invention went into rotation above his infuriating head. Jay made a grab for the nearest object — pretty nimble, I thought — but Wyr danced backwards several steps, somehow pulling his ill-gotten hoard with him.

I found myself almost as intrigued as I was furious. 'But you—' I said. 'You were nowhere near me!' How had he taken anything from my bag, not only without my noticing but without being within ten feet of me?

'Tell you what,' he said. 'Give me the unicorn. I'll not only let you have all these back, I'll show you how I purloined them in the first place. You could use a few survival skills.'

'I can't give you the unicorn,' I grated. 'She isn't for sale.'

'You mean... you lied?' Wyr turned a shocked countenance upon me. 'But at least you aren't a *thief* or something. That would be really bad.'

I groped in my shoulder-bag. To my relief, Mauf was still in there; too big and heavy to steal, perhaps. But the sleep-spheres I'd cadged from Orlando were not.

Hm.

Lucky that Jay and Emellana had kept the lyre out of Wyr's sight.

And I still had my pipes. Next time Jay was inclined to mock me for my choice of storage space, I'd thank him to remember this day. I had them out in a trice, but before I could play more than three notes, Emellana charged in, her mouth set in a thin, furious line, and levelled a crashing punch at Wyr's face.

It bounced off... something. Jay's attempt to grab the little creep fared much the same.

'Nice try,' Wyr grinned. 'But when you're this short, you learn a trick or two.'

I had to admit to a grudging respect for his shielding abilities. I wasn't bad at wards, but *I* couldn't have stopped that punch.

'Nice pipes,' said Wyr — and then, in the blink of an eye, they too were circling over Wyr's head in sequence with the scroll-case, the Wand, and Orlando's unnameable thing.

'Wha—' I spluttered. 'Give. Those. Back.'

My advance upon Wyr, violence filling my heart, was as ill-fated as Emellana's. But it was satisfying to try.

'Listen,' Wyr said. 'It's been blindingly obvious from the moment I met you that you lot are… something else. I don't know where you're from, but you're far out of your depth in Vale. I could run rings around you all day long. Not only that, but so could *every single person here,* so if you'd kindly get me that unicorn, you can have your stuff back, and I'll be on my way.'

I didn't love the feeling of helplessness those words created. He was right, and we knew it. I had only to think back to our utter incapacity to cope with the magickal surges of Old Farringale; if it weren't for the potions Emellana had procured, we'd be in a similar state now.

That said, perhaps we weren't far off it. Our wits must have been asleep ever since we'd set foot in the so-called Vales of Wonder, or we'd have got rid of Wyr already.

Even now, I couldn't seem to think how to proceed. My brain whirled in fuzzy circles and nothing came up.

'If you want the unicorn,' said Jay, 'she'll need those pipes back.'

Wyr's head tilted, and one brow went up. 'Oh?'

'Wait,' I said. 'Why do you want that particular unicorn anyway? I mean, look.' I made a sweeping gesture, which took in all the paddocks before us. 'You want a unicorn, take your pick.' We stood not six feet away from a long, silvery fence which shimmered with magick, and behind it there must have been fifty unicorns at least. What a glorious sight they made, too, for they came in every imaginable colour. So much ancient magick was compressed into that small space, the air itself pulsed and glimmered with it.

And that was just one of the many paddocks. The horizon was a mass of colour and magick.

I spotted Miranda, hanging half over the fence, her fingers entangled in the mane of a lavender-and-white unicorn, and sighed. Thanks for the help.

That look of utter disbelief was back on Wyr's face. 'Do you not even know *that* much?' he said incredulously. 'Honestly, where *did* you dig yourselves up from?'

'Far, far away,' I said impatiently. 'Someone said something about royal lines—'

'Yes,' Wyr all but shouted. 'Unicorns there are aplenty, but this lot's common as muck. Great for horns, teeth, bones, and so on, but I can't remember the last time anybody saw a pure-bred Majestic!' He was yelling now, but even at top volume, the word "Majestic" emerged with particular emphasis. 'And you were just *wandering around with it.* I'm amazed you kept it for as long as you did.'

His words ignited a miniature panic somewhere in my belly, for he was speaking *past tense,* and considering how long it was since any of us had caught a glimpse of Addie, perhaps he had a point. I'd assumed she was safer out of sight, and that I could call her back with a blast of my pretty pipes. But what if I couldn't?

What if someone had made off with her?

14

'I'M REALLY GOING TO need those pipes,' I said in a smouldering voice. I'm surprised I didn't set fire to Wyr's stupid hat.

'Like I said,' he answered. 'I'll trade you.'

'You don't understand. I can't get her back without those pipes.'

Wyr, at last, stopped juggling. 'You mean to say,' he said slowly, 'that these pipes can summon Majestics?'

'No. Just one particular one, and only if I do it.'

'How convenient.' He patently did not believe me.

A flicker of colour caught my eye. Some small, darting thing dived down upon Wyr, and flashed away again.

And the Wand was gone from his grasp.

'What?' His head came up, the pipes momentarily forgotten. Eyes narrowed, he looked hard at me. 'How did you do that?'

'You figure it out,' I said, with a smile. Let him chew on that.

Meanwhile, Miranda — for it had been *she* — whispered something to the bright blue bird in her grasp, and let it fly again.

This time, it returned with Orlando's glassy-looking toy.

Wyr's quick gaze caught some part of its return flight, for he whirled in Miranda's direction. 'You've got to be kidding me,' he spluttered. 'A Majestic and a gods-blessed *lirrabird*?'

I turned a questioning gaze upon Miranda, for I'd heard that name before. Lirrabirds were listed in Dramary's Bestiary. They were as fast as hummingbirds and not much larger, but remarkably strong for their diminutive size, and they responded well to training. They were sometimes referred to as the little winged wizards, because — as this one had just demonstrated — they were highly magickal, and difficult to deter by wizardly means. They'd made quite the pests of themselves among magickal communities, some few hundred years ago.

They were also extinct, at least on our Britain.

And now Miranda had a pet one.

'Ancestria Magicka pays well, hm?' I said.

'You're one to talk,' said Miranda. 'Do you know what I would have given for a tame unicorn?'

Ack. Had my friendship with Addie somehow fuelled Miranda's dissatisfaction? Was *I* part of the reason why she'd jumped ship?

I shook off the thought. Now wasn't the time to try to explain how Adeline and I had come about. 'Handy,' I offered instead, for to be fair, that lirrabird *had* just saved our hides.

Miranda gave a crooked smile, and tossed my pipes to me. 'You know,' she said, 'you could ask Addie what she'd like done about Wyr.'

'I reckon she wouldn't like him much,' I said, tightly clutching my pipes.

Miranda's smile widened. 'I reckon the same.'

So I lifted my precious pipes to my lips and I played Addie's song.

And I waited.

She didn't come.

'So much for the pipes,' muttered Wyr. He looked about at all of us with an expression much aggrieved, and added, 'And so much for the easy *mark*.' With which words, he stalked off, back towards the town.

'Good riddance,' I said, emulating Emellana's inhuman calm, though my insides were tying themselves in knots.

What had become of Addie? 'Question,' I said, as Miranda handed my Wand back to me. 'What did he mean about horns, teeth and bones?'

'Wondering the same thing,' said Miranda laconically, and turned a worried gaze upon the herd of unicorns behind us. 'You know, these... they're odd, too. See how still they are?'

She was right; they were as placid as cows, if not more so. They had a listless look about them. 'Wingless, all of them,' I observed.

'Makes sense if you want to hang onto them,' said Miranda, her frown deepening.

'Though we saw some winged ones, near the hill,' I said. 'Right?' We hadn't seen any since.

'It looks like a farm,' said Jay. 'Unicorn... milk?'

'Milk, and hairs from the manes and tails,' I said, remembering snippets of lore from the days of yore, back when unicorns had been more common in our Britain, too. Though there'd never been enough of them for entire farming operations, nor had they ever been... tamed, enough.

This was something else.

'Milk, hair,' said Miranda darkly. 'Horns, bones and teeth. Every part of a unicorn is magick-drenched, isn't it?'

'That's why they're so rare at home,' Jay said. 'Griffins, too — all the ancient mythicals, the deeply magickal creatures. Kings building thrones out of unicorn horns, people paying small fortunes for strands of unicorn hair or griffin claws or dragon's teeth, blood, scales... a damned rotten trade.'

We looked in silence at the listless herds of unicorns locked into their little paddocks, and I began to wonder. Was the fifth Britain more intensely magickal because they *hadn't* slaughtered all their most magickal creatures, the way we had? Or was it because they had taken the general idea, and run with it? Was it because they'd taken to farming their griffins and unicorns and dragons — not just for their potent bodily components, but also for their inherent magicks?

I began to find the wondrous Vale a fraction less charming.

Troubled about Addie, heartsick about the farms, I packed my purloined possessions back into my bag — and came up an item short. 'Mir, the scroll-case?'

Miranda blinked, and glanced down at her own hands, as though she might find herself still carrying it. 'Um, didn't I already give that to you?'

I double-checked. 'No. I've got the Wand, the panic button, Mauf, my pipes...'

'It isn't on me,' said Miranda, looking stricken.

'Your bird definitely got it back?'

'Yes.'

I glanced at Emellana, and Jay. 'Anybody else got it?'

They both shook their heads. 'Wyr?' Jay growled.

Doubtless. 'Damn that little sneak,' I sighed. 'No wonder he wandered off.'

'He'll be on the other side of bloody Vale by now,' said Jay.

Emellana looked more thoughtful than outraged. 'Now, why did he take that one article, and not the others?' she said.

'Because it's smothered in jewels?' I offered.

'Does that not seem mundane, as an attraction for a person like Wyr?' said Em. 'He struck me as consistently more interested in objects of magickal or arcane significance.'

Like "Majestic" unicorns, for example. 'But the scroll-case hasn't a scrap of magick about it,' I said. 'Has it?'

'Not that I could discern,' said Emellana. 'Nor has it ever been the subject of any past magicks.'

'That may not be true for much longer,' said Jay.

I raised a brow in his general direction.

'Well, what can Wyr want with it?' he said. 'It's of no use as a map, and I don't see why he would need one anyway. He's obviously very familiar with Vale. It's got to be something to do with its provenance. He played down the significance of Furgidan the Dispossessed, even in Vale, but he could've been lying.'

'I'd say that one never told a word of truth in his life, if he could help it,' I muttered, and gave a sigh. 'So we need to get that back. Along with my poor lost Adeline, and *then* we can proceed with the mission.' I had to think for a moment to remember what that even was.

Torvaston's expedition to the Vales of Wonder. What, where, when, how, and why.

Right.

I shook my head to clear it, without much success. 'How long do those potions last?'

Emellana looked at me. 'Your hair's growing flowers again.'

'I was afraid of that.' I hefted my shoulder bag. 'Next stop, the potion shop,' I said, and made it two steps before my darling pup came running up, ears perky, tail furiously a-wag.

She had a severed unicorn horn in her mouth.

'Oh,' I said upon a long sigh, and took it from her. 'Thanks, pup.'

Little Goodie Goodfellow grinned a huge puppy grin at me, immensely pleased with herself.

THE POTION SHOP WAS actually called, with rather greater sophistication, Benbollen's Elixir Emporium, and to call it eye-opening would be to sadly understate the case. I wondered how Emellana had kept her implacable cool, turned loose in the place by herself not long since, for it was like walking into a sweet-shop at the approximate age of five. *What* had that woman even seen, in her long, long life, to be so unimpressed? For the shop was vastly larger on the inside than it had any right to be, considering the very modest proportions we'd glimpsed from outside. It was also... taller. Far taller. The ceiling was up there somewhere, I could almost swear it. But, like the library at Mandridore, it was far distant, and obscured by floating wisps of cloud.

Every wall was crammed with shelves, and every shelf was crowded with elixirs. They were presented in bottles of every size, shape and material — not just glass, ladies and gents, because why stop there? These were amethyst and onyx and granite and silver and a host of substances I couldn't identify. Those that were clear displayed potions of every possible colour, many of them unusually active. They swirled and rippled and bubbled and glittered and spun in their elegant bottles, and I could've cheerfully stayed all year until I'd had chance to try every single one of them. Or at least to learn what they did.

Seldom have I seen such a wealth of colour... and magickal possibility.

I inched nearer to Emellana, who stood with her usual poise in the centre of the shop floor, glancing occasionally at some potion or another with an expression of polite interest. She could not be so totally unmoved as she appeared. *Surely.*

'Ever seen anything like this at home?' I asked her.

'No,' she said, but then added, 'Well. The markets at Cairo in the thirties were remarkable. More informally presented, of course, but full of marvels.'

'Were?' I echoed.

'It's all gone now.' I thought I saw a trace of regret in her calm features, but couldn't be sure.

For the first time, it occurred to me that Emellana was old enough to have seen some of our world's magickal decline first hand. What had the world of her youth been like? I opened my mouth to ask, but shook my head. *Not the time, Ves. Practical matters first.* 'Forgive me,' I said, 'but how did you pay for the first batch of potions?'

Her eyes gleamed with something like... amusement? A trace of smugness? But she only said: 'The same way I paid for your pot. Your pup is an enterprising creature. She dug up a jewel not half an hour ago, which the shopkeeper appeared to consider valuable.'

I wondered briefly why pup had chosen to make Emellana the beneficiary of her peculiar brand of largesse, and let the thought go. If pup was as much inclined as I was to develop a mild crush on the magnificent older lady, I could hardly blame her.

And she *had* brought me the prize article, even if it was one I did not especially welcome. I retrieved the horn from my bag, trying not to look at its ragged, bloodied end. The damned thing was freshly harvested. 'Do you think they'd accept a barter?'

A flicker of distaste crossed Emellana's face as she looked at the horn. 'Yes, let us dispose of it.'

I approached the proprietor, an elfin lady younger and shorter than myself, with the kind of bright, slightly fixed smile common to practiced shop assistants everywhere. 'Welcome to Benbollen's,' she said cheerfully.

'Hi,' I said. 'I gather you sold this lady a batch of potions earlier today.' I indicated Emellana with a wave of my hand. Something had caught her attention and she'd wandered off.

'Four doses of Tylerin's Suppressants?' she said promptly. Her gaze took in the flowers bobbing gently in my hair.

'Right. Can I get a repeat order of that? Two, even, if this is sufficient to cover it.' I displayed the severed horn.

'Absolutely,' she said, to my relief. 'Did you want only the two? That's enough alicorn to make four or five batches.'

15

I wondered if I'd heard correctly. 'One second,' I said. 'To *make* four or five batches?'

'I'd think so. I mean, I'm not an alchemixer, but—'

'Tylerin's Suppressants are made out of unicorn horns?'

'The very finest,' she said, with horrible cheer. 'And every bottle's steeped in unicorn hair, and, um... traces of dragon blood... I've got the literature on it somewhere.'

I interrupted her search for a no doubt horrifically informative leaflet. 'That's okay, I don't need to read about it.'

She stopped searching, and thankfully took the horn from me. 'So five batches, then?' she said.

I took a moment to grope for words, and to dispense with the raging I was sorely tempted to embark upon. 'I

157

don't quite… I mean, how is it a suppressant if the stuff pumps us full of magickal elements?'

'I know it seems confusing, but it's really very clever,' she enthused. 'Tylerin theorised that the effects of Vale, and other potent sources of magick, are due to an imbalance between the environment and the subject. You're over-whelmed because you yourself are significantly *less* mag-ickal than your surroundings. Do you see? So the suppres-sant actually bumps up your magick rating until it's more comparable with the environment, and then you can move through even a strong magickal surge more or less safely.'

'More or less,' I repeated.

'These are calibrated for Vale,' she said. 'We sell a range of grades adjusted for body mass and magickal talent, but unless you get a dose custom-made for yourself there'll be some variation in the results.' She brightened. 'Would you like custom doses? Our best alchemixer is in today, and she'd be delighted to assist you.'

'No!' I said, backing away. Whatever the consequences might prove to be, I couldn't bring myself to imbibe any more of Benbollen's wondrous elixirs now that I knew what went into them.

'I mean, I know it's not much different from eating a burger, when I happen to think well of cows,' I said a little later to Jay, once we stood in a mildly disconsolate knot on the pavement outside the shop. 'I still can't bring myself to drink any more of it.'

I observed what appeared to be a suppressed shudder in Jay. 'That's sort of why I don't eat burgers,' he said. 'But I take your point.'

'You... you don't?'

Jay shook his head. 'Vegetarian.'

I blinked. 'I feel I ought to have noticed that before now.'

He grinned. 'I don't really expect you to pay that much attention to my quirks.'

'This place is *vile,*' said Miranda with energy, erupting from the shop behind us. She had remained behind, for the pleasure of wrangling with the shop assistant. I doubted her attempts at remonstrating with them over the morality of their business had been productive of much. She stalked past us into the street, stiff with rage.

'Have they seen the error of their ways?' I called after her.

She merely bristled — visibly — and declined to answer.

Emellana smiled faintly, and said nothing.

'We'd better work fast,' said Jay. 'If we aren't using any more suppressants. Or whatever they are.'

'Right.' I forced my spinning brain to focus. 'Griffins. Torvaston. Magickal surges. Um...' I hauled Mauf out of my bag and wandered after Miranda, keeping half an eye out for... cars? No. We hadn't seen hide nor hair of a car in all of the fifth Britain. 'Mauf, have you had chance to brush up on Torvaston's magnum opus?'

'The fragmentary sections of it you have yet seen fit to give me?' said Mauf. 'Yes, madam.'

'The rest is coming, I swear, whenever the scholars at Mandridore have finished translating it. Is there anything juicy in what we've got?'

'Anything on the topic of griffins in particular,' Jay put in.

'Or unicorns,' I added. 'Dragons, any such creatures.'

'It distresses me more than I can express to disappoint you, madam,' said Mauf, apparently ignoring Jay. 'But there is little on those subjects among the lost king's notes.'

'Notes?' I echoed. 'I thought this was his great work of scholarship. And therefore, you know, finished.'

'Perhaps it may prove to be, once I receive the rest. But the majority of the material I have yet received is in note form.'

'Very well. Can you give us a precis of what it says?'

'*Farringale is a source of some of the purest and most potent magick I have ever encountered,*' quoted Mauf, and added as an aside, 'I paraphrase, madam, you understand.'

'I do indeed. Paraphrase away. We're in a hurry.'

'Right.' Mauf cleared his throat. '*In full flow, it is like an ocean; an unstoppable tide, engulfing all in its wake. And yet, it does not destroy. It empowers. Those whose strength and might are such as to permit them to harness such a force — of what may such magicians not prove capable? The most remarkable feats of magick lie within our grasp, if only we can learn to ride these waves. Imagine the prospects! Our Britain, transformed by magick.*

'I look into the future, and see — decline. This must not be. I will not permit it. The means to avert this future lie in my own hands; of this I am certain. And Farringale is, must be, the key.'

Mauf paused in his recitation. 'There is a deal more in this general style, madam, but I would not judge that it serves to illuminate the matter further. I shall skip to...' He paused, and I pictured him mentally leafing through pages. 'Ah. There is a single mention of "great birds", which we may take, with reasonable confidence, to mean the griffins; but I should not like to be quoted upon that.'

'Understood, Mauf.'

'The great birds of Mount Farringale dwindle in number,' continued Mauf. *'Even as the tides of magick dissipate. In my lifetime alone, the ocean has become a sea; in future years, shall there be nothing of it left? What is the reason for this decline? I make it my life's work to understand its causes, and to reverse it. This I vow.'*

'I wonder,' I mused. 'Was that how Farringale came to fall? Did Torvaston try to reverse the decline, and succeed a little too well?'

'His notes do not yet make that clear, madam,' said Mauf.

'Is there anything about another Britain?' Emellana put in.

'I am getting to that, my lady,' said Mauf coldly.

'My apologies,' said Emellana, gravely, but with a small smile.

Mauf sniffed. 'There is a degree of waffle on the subject of *other shores*. Ahem. *So like Farringale, and yet so other. Here magick fades; there it burgeons. What crucial differences render the patterns thus? In what fashion do we fail? The answers lie otherwhere, and thither I go.*'

'He could have been talking about any place,' I said. 'He never mentions another world.'

'No, but he has not mentioned a city either,' said Emellana. 'We may fairly conclude that he was speaking of this Britain. We do know, beyond reasonable doubt, that he came here.'

She was right. *Don't go looking for complications, Ves.* 'Is that it, Mauf?' I said.

'That is *it,* as you put it. At least, I doubt that you are much interested in his musings on his own personal state of health, or his growing dependency on the *magickal flow,* as he puts it.'

'We might be. What does he say?'

'Briefly,' put in Jay. 'In a hurry, recall.' I'd been so focused on what Mauf was saying that I hadn't paid much attention to where we were going. Fortunately, Jay had, and I was so used to wandering along in his wake that I had followed him without thinking. We had left the Elixir Emporium behind, and much of the town with it. The mountain around whose base Vale was built loomed before us, bigger with every step we took. Miranda had her gaze fixed firmly upon the distant, wheeling figures far above us, and I remembered what she'd said about the oddities of their flight patterns.

'Mir,' I began, but changed my mind when she did not look round. Time for that later. 'Sorry,' I said to Mauf, collecting my scattered wits. 'What does Torvaston say about dependency?'

'A deal about the *sweet, intense sensations,*' answered Mauf. 'It seems he developed a habit of being mountain-side whenever the surges happened, for he deemed that *the centre.* Indeed, in perusing his notes I wonder whether he spent much time anywhere else, after a while.' Mauf was speaking very rapidly, Jay's urgency infecting him. 'He began it in hopes of better understanding the nature of the flow, and discovering a way to improve its potency once more. He may not have been aware himself of its increasing hold over him; his coherence decreases in such a fashion as to lead me to suspect that he was...'

'What?' I prompted, when Mauf trailed off.

'Losing his marbles, I believe is the phrase?'

'Ah. Well. Considering our own less than stellar perfor-mances when under the influence of an extreme magickal *flow*, I wouldn't be surprised. If you're not used to it, it's...'

'Intense,' offered Jay.

'*Sweet,*' I added, and swayed. My hair was a mass of flow-ers. Jay sported a short, gleaming-white pair of horns peek-ing from among his tousled black hair. Miranda looked to be growing wings, though she was not yet aware, except for perhaps an itching sensation at her shoulder-blades, for she kept rolling her shoulders in irritable fashion.

Emellana, as ever, appeared unaffected.

I really wondered about her.

'Mauf,' said Emellana, even as I formed the thought.

'Yes, my lady.'

'You have spent some little time in close quarters with that lost scroll-case, have you not?'

'Yes, my lady. I found it an uncouth companion, much puffed up in its own conceit.'

'Indeed?' One white brow lifted. 'Why is that, do you imagine?'

'In the way of books, scrolls and other such volumes,' said Mauf, 'there can be no denying that the case is espe-cially well-dressed.'

'You refer to the jewels.'

'Yes, my lady. Furthermore, it appeared to think itself a composition of enormous importance.' Mauf's tone grew indignant. 'And this in spite of the fact that it boasted an array of mere *scribblings,* from the pen of an incompetent scribe! I would be embarrassed to call myself a *work*!'

'Curious,' Emellana remarked. 'It did not happen to share with you its reasons for imagining itself so significant?'

'No, my lady.' Mauf hesitated. 'I found its manner obnoxious, and did not encourage its further acquaintance. I apologise if I have thus erred.'

'I do not imagine I would have acted differently,' she said graciously.

'Thank you, madam.'

'Interesting,' I said. 'And I could have sworn it had nothing on it but a hastily-outlined map of the Vales.'

'And the Hyndorin Mountains,' Jay reminded me.

'Yes, though... it did not seem, in either case, that anything of note was marked upon it. Did it?'

Jay was frowning, shook his head. 'Not that I recall.'

'Would you perhaps like to verify the information?' Mauf offered.

'Wait,' I said, stopping in the middle of a placid residential street full of sleepy bungalows. 'What?'

'I believe I can recall the details of the maps, if you should like to see them again.'

'Yes!' I said. 'Yes, please. Definitely.' I opened Mauf's covers to the first blank page he had, and waited.

16

THE THICK, CREAMY PAPER shimmered, and lines etched in black ink began to appear, snaking across the pages. Torvaston's map of the Vales of Wonder was first rendered, and then the ragged outlines of a mountain range. Helpful as Mauf's recreation was, I still couldn't see anything on it that would explain Wyr's apparent interest.

But one thought did enter my head.

'Mountains,' I said, and pointed at the one before us (even if it was only a tall hill, in truth).

'What?' said Jay.

'Griffins. Wherever we've seen griffins, we've seen high ground.'

'We've only seen griffins twice.'

'I know, but—'

'Twice could be a coincidence. You need three for a pattern.'

'Fine. I'll bet you a stack of pancakes as tall as that *hill* that these Hyndorin Mountains are stuffed full of griffins.'

'That,' said Jay, looking way, way up, 'would be a lot of pancakes.'

'I am confident of winning.'

'To say the least.'

'And that would make three, wouldn't it?'

'Mm. I think I won't take that bet.'

'Jay! Why not?'

'Because if you eat that many pancakes you'll explode, and we need you.'

I smirked. 'You know I'd win, too.'

'I suspect you might be onto something, let's put it that way.'

We were fast approaching the base of the hill, now. Vale had been built right up against it; some of its houses were built straight into the hillside. 'I get the impression this town was once more populous than it is now,' I said. 'It's too big for its population.'

'Could be,' Jay agreed. 'This has to be the old quarter.'

He was right, or so I judged. The houses nearer the great hill were timber-framed structures, though not all of them would own up to the fact. Some sported stucco frontages in improbable colours, and like the newer parts of the town, they were... unusually animated. Chimney pots sprouted from roofs and exploded into clouds of dust; a grasshopper sitting upon the step of one such home suddenly expanded to thirty times its regular size, chirruped loudly, and shrank again; one house grew bored of its ground floor, apparently, and shifted the rooms upwards, taking a stretching set of steps up with it.

'Are they actually doing all that?' I said plaintively. 'Or is it me that's deranged, and all this is going on in my own head?'

'That cottage is growing a hat,' said Jay calmly. 'It's a blue stovepipe, and there's smoke coming out of — oh, it's a chimney.'

A glance verified these words to be perfect truth, but I wasn't altogether sure that made it any better. 'Moving swiftly on,' I said.

Miranda was way ahead of us, already climbing the hill, her legs pumping. Did she mean to power straight to the top? 'Ves!' she suddenly yelled, turning. 'Get up here!'

'What?' I shouted back. 'Why?'

She was pointing, up and behind me. I spun — and saw a familiar-looking winged unicorn swooping past far overhead, though where she had acquired that shell-pink colour I couldn't have said. It was certainly Addie, though. For one, she was still wearing the silvery harness. For another... it's been ten years for us. I'd know her anywhere, whatever colour she wore.

I began to run, pulling my pipes out of my shirt as I went. It's not easy to run uphill and play a wind instrument at the same time, let me tell you, but such was my relief at seeing Adeline hale and unharmed that I spared no effort. By the time I reached Miranda I was winded and, most likely, lobster-red in the face, but I was playing Addie's song with every scrap of breath I could muster.

She heard me. I don't know how I could tell, but I had no doubt.

She didn't come down.

'She's up there for a reason,' I said, relief giving way to curiosity.

'She's not the only one,' said Miranda. 'I've counted five winged unicorns up there since we left the Emporium. Ves, they're as messed up as the griffins. Look. Watch her.'

We stood there for some time, watching intently as Adeline soared far over our heads. Mir was right: others joined the aerial dance from time to time, weaving in and out of Addie's path with such perfect grace, the display looked... choreographed. And Addie was part of it.

'The griffins are the same,' said Miranda after a while.

Jay joined us, Emellana leaning on his arm. Formidable she might be, but a steep hill proved a challenge after all. For some reason, I was reassured by this sign of ordinary mortal weakness — and glad we had Jay to think of things like that. All thought but of Addie had gone out of my head.

'It is some kind of enchantment, holding them there,' said Emellana, slightly breathlessly. 'I can feel it, even from down here.'

I looked keenly at her. 'Why?'

'It is a familiar magick, to me. It is a variation on a series of charms sometimes used at Mandridore.'

'Where at Mandridore?'

She returned my gaze in silence for so long, I thought she would not answer. But at last she said: 'The Royal Menagerie.'

'There's a Royal Menagerie?'

'It is not a matter for public knowledge,' said Emellana. 'The creatures there are highly endangered, and, I need hardly add, highly valuable.'

'What creatures?' I said. 'This is important, Em.'

'There are three unicorns, two of them winged. One griffin, though she is of such age, it is not thought that she will live more than another few years. Dragons of several species, two of them pygmy. A lirrabird, such as Miranda now possesses.' She inclined her head in Mir's direction. 'A goldnose, like your pup; that is a very new acquisition. In fact, we have a breeding pair. Assorted other species, I need not name them all. Suffice it to say that it is the broadest, and rarest, collection of its type in Europe.' She amended that to, 'In *our* Europe.'

It crossed my mind to wonder how the Court had got hold of a pair of goldnoses, until I remembered Alban. He'd had one or two secret assignments out at the fifth that he hadn't shared with me, hm?

Jay said, 'And they're under enchantment?'

'Minor behavioural influences, that is all,' said Emellana. 'A pacifying charm, commonly used by those of Miranda's profession. They are not controlled, precisely, but they are... encouraged in certain directions.' She nodded at the unicorns winging over our heads, and the griffins farther beyond. 'This is a much, much stronger version of it.'

'But what are they being compelled to do?' I said. 'They're just circling.'

'If I may be permitted,' said Emellana. 'I'd like to use the lyre.'

'It isn't mine,' I said bluntly.

But she was looking at Jay.

'Ves needs to be protected,' he said.

'Hey,' I objected. 'I'm standing right here.'

He ignored me. 'She's at risk from the lyre, in ways we don't yet understand.'

'I don't need protecting,' I growled.

'Don't take it personally,' Jay said, briefly squeezing my hand. 'Everyone needs help from time to time.'

'Fine,' I sighed. 'What are you doing with the lyre, Em?'

'I intend to ascend to the summit,' she said. 'I suspect that most major, truly compelling magicks in this town have been performed from up there, particularly those affecting the beasts hereabouts. I would like to read the traces. But we are dealing with ancient, unusually potent magicks, and I will require aid. The lyre is the tool I need.'

Not for the first time, I wondered at Milady's apparent ability to anticipate the needs of any given assignment unusually early, and to arrange for their being available. Once or twice, I'd almost plucked up the courage to ask her if there were by chance any fortune-tellers in her family tree. But I never had. It's not like she'd tell me the truth if I did.

Meanwhile, we had more immediate problems. I tilted back my head, shading my eyes against an insistent drizzle of rain, and took a good, long look at just how far away the summit was. The hill might have been only a hill, not a true mountain, but it would still take us over an hour's solid climbing to reach the top. And Emellana was a thousand years old. 'Forgive me,' I said to her. 'But you can't climb that.'

'No,' she agreed, smiling. 'I was thinking the same thing.'

'We need chairs,' said Jay, looking around, as though he might see an abandoned dining set standing forlornly amidst the rubble and bracken of the hillside.

I said nothing, assailed by a feeling of disquiet. We were in a hurry, too much of a hurry to go trawling back down the hill looking for chairs to thieve. And we were in such a hurry because the deep, deep magicks of Vale were getting the better of us, minute by minute. The effects might yet be mostly cosmetic, but that would change. I did not want to be halfway up the hill, airborne and in charge of a tricky array of charms to keep us that way, when the magicks of Vale overwhelmed my sanity.

But how else could we ascend the hill, if we couldn't climb and we couldn't fly?

I conveyed some of this.

'Right,' said Jay. 'True. Okay. But, this is the fifth Britain. The henge complexes, and the bubble transports, tell us that there's major magickal infrastructure. And if Emellana is right, and a lot of important stuff has happened at the peak, then what are the chances that someone's installed an easier way to the top by now?'

'High!' I enthused.

'It will be at the bottom,' said Jay.

I stared in mild dismay at the distance between us and the ground. Hard-won, in Emellana's case. 'Down we go, then,' I said heartily, and off we went. Rain made for damp ground, and our progress was more of a slither-and-slide than a stout trek, but we made it back to town-level in one piece. Or indeed, four pieces.

It was Jay's happy thought to cut down on the searching by snagging the first passerby he saw: a reassuringly ordinary-looking man, with only a glowing jewel through his nose to remind us of where we were.

'The peak?' he repeated.

I did not at all see why this concept was proving hard to grasp, but I pointed upwards, just to be clear. 'The peak,' I agreed.

He blinked at us. 'You're sure?'

'Why... wouldn't we be?' I said.

His smile was faint. 'There's a lift,' he said. 'Around that way.' He indicated a winding path that snaked away to my right.

'Thank you, kind sir.'

Jay didn't budge. 'Is there anything up there we should know about?' he asked.

Our friendly interlocutor shrugged. 'All the things you'd go up the peak *for*, correct?' With which superlatively unhelpful statement, he turned away, and left us to our fate.

'Apparently,' I said, with a winsome smile, 'we look like people who know what we're doing.'

Jay looked from me, to Miranda, to Emellana, palpably in doubt. 'Uh huh.'

I had to see his point. Emellana might have an air of formidable wisdom, but she *was* rather elderly, and looking tired to boot. Miranda looked more distracted even than usual, her clothes were in holes, and moths were crawling out of her hair.

As for me, who knew? But I had a feeling that a head full of flowers was only the beginning.

'We're people who know what we're doing,' I repeated more firmly.

Jay nodded. 'And if you say something often enough, it becomes true.'

'Always.'

I looked up and up, gazing for a moment at the distant heights of the mini-mountain before us. The rain returned, dropping fat, chilly droplets into my eyes. 'Addie's up there,' I said.

'Together with a lot of other beasts that need our help,' Miranda added.

Jay nodded, and squared his shoulders. 'Are we ready for this?'

'Let me at 'em,' I said.

He smiled, but without mirth. 'Then up we go.'

17

I DON'T KNOW THAT I want to describe what Vale means by the term "lift". Let's just say that the inhabitants of that fine town have stronger stomachs than you or I.

We were... conveyed... to the summit of (for lack of a better name for it) Mount Vale, and when we had finished shrieking (me), gibbering (Miranda), cursing (surprisingly, Jay), and shaking (Emellana), we were at leisure to notice a few things about it.

One: the wind. One might expect a high wind up at such a height, certainly, but the hair-tossing, screaming, ferocious wind we encountered up there was... shall I call it vindictive? I stood braced at the summit, the peculiar, motley town of Vale spread far below me, hanging onto my shirt for grim death because the damned mischievous mistral seemed intent upon wresting it from me.

'Everyone all right?' I yelled over the noise, and I'm fairly sure no one heard so much as a syllable.

Two: Unusual light conditions. The afternoon was wearing on by then, but it shouldn't have been anywhere near dark yet. At the top of Mount Vale, though, a deep, glimmering twilight reigned, and attractive as it was, I found the effect foreboding.

Three: magick. I ought perhaps to have mentioned that first, because Emellana's instincts were promptly proved more or less right. If Vale in general was a magick-drowned town, up *there* was the centre, the source of it all, and no wonder the light and the weather weren't right. Nothing could be, in a mess like that. Magick thrummed through the ground beneath my feet, and set my bones vibrating. Magick made my head swim and my heart pound; magick made me mighty and weak, shallow and profound, pink and purple— no, lost the train of thought. Magick. Made it difficult to think clearly.

I shut my eyes for a while, hoping by that means to force my disordered brain to focus.

It worked. Sort of.

What we didn't find up there was much of anything *but* wind and whimsy and gloaming. Unsurprising, perhaps? What manner of structure could survive such conditions? If it withstood the weird weather, it couldn't resist the magick. Five minutes, and it would make a bubble of itself and float away, or stalk back down the mountain again on chicken legs.

I mean, anything was possible up there. Anything.

There were griffins, though.

Oh my, were there griffins.

I've been up close and personal with a griffin or two before. You may recall. The first time, I was convinced I was about to get eaten, and didn't get much chance to examine the creature. The second time was better, but still... I've never been so close to a griffin before, nor had such leisure to admire it.

They're beautiful, and terrifying. Majestic. Magnificent. Vast, all muscle and feather and hide, wreathed in magick of a potency I couldn't have dreamed of only a few weeks ago.

And that was bad, because Mir was right: these creatures were *wrong.* They wafted past us on the wing, utterly oblivious to our presence, dancing upon those currents of air with the grace of butterflies. Lightning — not light at all, but raw, intense magick — glittered around them, darting from wing to wing, crackling over their backs and igniting their claws with white fire. There was far too much there, far, *far* more than the griffins of Farringale had borne. And still they ignored us.

We stood in awed silence for a time, watching as those mighty beasts circled slowly around the summit of Mount

Vale, and around us, standing motionless at its centre. And I realised that the winds and the griffins danced in tandem, and in a pattern perfectly regular. Like automated figures on a cuckoo-clock, their perfect circuit never varied.

Strong enchantments, indeed.

I realised that Jay was attempting to get my attention. This occurred to me only when he put his lips two inches away from my left ear and yelled, 'Ves!'

'*What?*'

'Em's using the lyre,' he screamed. 'Forgive me.'

He swept me up in a brutal... embrace, I couldn't quite call it, for it was restraining, not affectionate. His hands clamped over my eyes, blocking out my view of those magnificent griffins. My objections went unheeded, and Jay proved as strong as an ox; nothing that I did loosened his grip one bit.

I was grateful for it a few moments later, for whatever Em was doing with that lyre was... like nothing I've ever experienced before. Emellana Rogan began to play; the ancient lyre's thrumming notes sounded over the arcane winds at Mount Vale; and around me, the world went insane.

It began with a heightening of the already mad winds, until a veritable cyclone spun around and around us. Only, some part of it must have been no wind at all, or we would have been swept up into the skies. A sensation as of powerful currents tore at my clothes and my hair and howled in my ears; over the tumult, I distantly heard a griffin shriek.

Then came a tide of rain, like an ocean flipped upside down and poured upon our shrinking heads. My clothes clung to my skin, icy-cold, and I struggled to breathe through air turned to torrents of water. Colours flooded my mind, rain turned moon-pale and ice-white, eventide-blue and moss-green and every conceivable variation of hue, and shining like drowned stars. Did I imagine it? Throughout, the feel of Jay's hands tucked firmly over my eyes did not lessen, and still he held on.

Emellana's music turned haunting, morose. Its melody melded with the winds, took the rains inside itself and spun it out again in a ripple of strident notes.

I began to see things.

Visions filled my turbulent mind, sense and nonsense hopelessly jumbled together. I saw a litter of snow-white cubs with striped tails, which became goldnoses — all of them my pup, like little clones — and then they were changed to lirrabirds, like Miranda's. My mind's eye filled in with gleaming, tawny-amber colour, something that shimmered like polished jewels; downy feathers ringed the gleaming sphere, a mote of black at its centre, and I realised I stared deep into the eye of a griffin.

An enraged griffin. A fathomless anger was there, and a din filled my ears as of a thousand griffins screaming in unison.

A unicorn, its hide rippling in waves of shifting colours. Its horn vanished, reappeared, multiplied; wings sprouted and faded; it melted into a pool of pale water and disappeared.

A mighty troll took its place, a figure towering so high in my mind's eye that the world fell away before him. He wore a crown I'd seen before, and in his face was a granite resolve tinged with incipient madness.

I saw a tide of magick — a chaotic flood of colour, sound, light, cacophonic music — sweep over a Britain I knew, leaving nothing unchanged in its wake.

Is this what people come to the peak for? I thought, distantly, and dissolved into a mirth I knew to be inappropriate, but could not contain.

'It's all right, Ves,' Jay murmured in my ear, and I could hear him, though he spoke softly. The howl of the winds had died. 'Are you okay?'

I wasn't immediately sure how to answer. It took me three long seconds to remember that *Ves* was me, my own name, and the man behind me with his hands over my face was Jay, and we'd come to this place of shrieking insanity for a good reason.

What was it?

'It'll come to me,' I said aloud.

'I'll take that as no,' said Jay, though he carefully loosened the grip of one hand, and I regained a glimmer of sight in my right eye.

And hastily closed it again, tight, for the gloaming somehow blazed with light, more brightly than high noon, though it was a pallid rather than a vivid glow, and everything ethereally a-shimmer.

Emellana stood in the centre of it like a goddess, taller than seemed possible, and her eyes were afire with the same light.

The lyre, to my mixed disappointment and relief, was no longer in her hands, and the music was gone.

'So it's been an interesting half-hour,' I commented, as I waited for my seared eye to stop watering.

'Could say that,' Jay agreed.

I thought I heard someone sobbing. 'They're enslaved,' Miranda was saying. *'Slaves.'*

Who? I wanted to ask, but realisation dawned as my sluggish brain caught up, and I didn't need to. She meant the griffins, of course, and the unicorns.

Including my Adeline.

Emellana's shoulders sagged. She swayed like a young tree in the wind, and would have fallen had not Jay and I hastened to catch her. We helped her to sit down, and she did so without appearing to notice the seeping wet earth beneath her, or the wind driving rain into her eyes. 'I am very well,' she insisted, smiling up at us, and I wondered how much the deep magick of that place, and whatever she had done to it, had addled her brain. If at all.

'It is an old spot, you know,' she said after a little while, looking around at the gloomy hilltop. 'Ancient. Much older than Torvaston and his court. I found layers of magick running deep, so deep...' She stopped speaking, and stared mistily over the landscape. 'The griffins have always been here,' she continued at length. 'The griffins, and their like. The enchantments which bind them, however, are much newer.'

'How much newer?' I said.

'Measurements of time are arbitrary constructions,' she said, smiling vaguely at me. 'It is impossible to determine anything of that kind from the traces I have lately read. I could not say *this number of hundred years ago,* or *since that event.* I can only say, that they have permeated the earth and the air of this place, but not to any great depth.'

I thought about that. 'If I understand you rightly, you mean to say that they probably were not laid down by Torvaston, or anybody else, as much as four centuries ago.'

'Perhaps not, indeed,' Emellana agreed.

'But I saw him,' I said. 'At least, I am fairly sure it was him.'

Emellana's gaze turned upon me, and, at last, sharpened. 'Saw him?' she echoed.

'I had visions,' I elaborated, looking first at Em and then at Jay. 'Surely it wasn't just me?'

Jay just looked at me.

'Oh. Well, I saw... everything was very confused. I don't quite know what much of it was. Enraged griffins, chaotic unicorns, and a troll king...' I could dredge nothing more concrete out of my churning thoughts.

'A king?' said Jay. 'How do you know he was a king?'

'Because he was wearing a crown.'

'That would narrow it down,' Jay agreed.

'And we saw that crown in the museum at Farringale,' I continued.

'Are you certain?'

'Perfectly. Though, I cannot say that it means anything. I may have added that detail myself, or interpreted the crown in question as one that was familiar to me. It was a... confusing experience.'

Jay said, thoughtfully, 'That might be so. Otherwise, it's going to be hard to explain how you saw Torvaston *here* wearing a crown he left behind in the old Britain.'

'It could be a mental construction of Ves's own,' Emellana said, some of her old calm returning. 'Time will tell, I suspect.' She levered herself to her feet, leaning heavily upon me and upon Jay, and stood in silence for a moment.

I began to wonder what had become of Miranda, and my pup. The latter I saw trotting gaily through the rain, apparently untouched by it, though her fur was slicked with wet. It took rather more effort to locate Miranda. I saw her at last, far on the other side of the hill, a bedraggled, sopping-wet figure with her face turned up to the rain, searching the sky. She'd got as close as she could to the griffins, whose regular flight patterns brought them nearest to that side of the hill.

'Is she right?' I said, nodding in Miranda's direction. 'Are they truly enslaved?'

'Oh, yes,' said Emellana. 'It is not mere pacification, or coercion. They are absolutely bound, stripped of all independent thought, or capacity for independent action. It is the type of magick long banned in our Britain.'

'And here they're using it to farm ancient mythical creatures like cattle,' I said, feeling unusually grim. And it wasn't just because I was wet to the skin and I had snakes coiling in my hair.

18

'WE HAVE TO GET them out,' said Miranda, rejoining us. She was still bristling with fury, and stalked more than walked through the rain, her face a perfect thundercloud. 'We can't leave them like this.'

I hesitated, picturing the chaos we would create if we somehow broke the magickal bindings which held the griffins and their ilk spellbound. 'We—'

'Ves,' said Miranda. 'Help me or not as you choose, but I will not leave this town until these creatures are free.' Her fists balled as though she might hit me.

I raised my hands. 'Hey. We're on the same—' I stopped. I couldn't say we were on the same side anymore, because we... weren't. Were we? At least not technically. 'We have the same goals,' I said instead. 'I don't want to leave these poor beasts like this any more than you do — and I'm damned if I'll even think about leaving without Addie. But we have to think about this.'

Jay made a slight noise. When I glanced his way, he'd adopted an expression of bland innocence. 'I said nothing,' he informed me.

I made a face at him. 'I know I'm fond of barging in without thinking things through, and sometimes it's the best approach — you don't have time to *over* think, and basically talk yourself out of what has to be done. But you of all people know, Jay, that sometimes it's just insane. Isn't that what you keep telling me? And this is one of those times. This place is... way beyond us. We are far, far out of our magickal league here.'

'We could...' said Miranda, and stopped.

'Exactly,' I said. 'Em? Could you get anywhere near those enchantments? Even with the lyre?'

'I doubt it,' she said.

'Maybe we could do it together,' said Miranda, and looked at me with the eyes of hope. 'All four of us. We're strong as a group.'

Strong as a group. Fine words from the woman who'd very lately abandoned her group, and tossed us to the wolves to boot.

Not the time, Ves.

I pushed my ugly thoughts aside, and tried to consider the question on its own merits.

'Even as a group,' said Jay. 'We're outclassed. It's not even about quantity or potency of magick. Even if we were as strong in magick as the people here, we don't know what to do with it. It's beyond us in every conceivable way.'

He was right, painful though it always is to admit one's shortcomings.

A rather depressed silence fell. My eyes followed the passage of a far-off griffin as it soared helplessly upon the tossing winds.

'But,' said Emellana unexpectedly. 'We do know how to cause chaos.'

I looked at her.

'Or at least,' she amended, regarding me with a twinkle in her eyes, 'Ves does.'

Jay was ungentlemanly enough to smirk. 'Are you kidding? She's famous for it.'

'Positively legendary,' Emellana agreed.

'Hey,' I said. 'I'm standing right here.'

Jay beamed at me. 'And here's your chance to shine.'

'How would that even help?' I demanded. They weren't wrong. I probably could cause quite the ruckus, and the utter madness of the magick of Vale might aid rather than impede me. But what would it achieve?

'This is a system of perfect order,' said Jay. 'And it is beautifully done, perfectly maintained. Those beasts out there — the unicorns back on the farms — they could be clockwork pieces in a giant mechanical system. It's glorious. But the downside to such structures is, they do not adapt well.'

Emellana was nodding in agreement. 'The proverbial spanner in the works. Make enough of a mess, Ves, and I think we may see some interesting results.'

'And that,' Jay added, with a glance at Miranda, 'we may very well manage as a group.'

'With our lady of chaos to guide us,' said Emellana, bowing her head in my direction.

I wasn't sure I liked what bordered upon aspersions upon my character, but since I could hardly argue that they were unjust, I let it pass. 'I'm as willing to make a mess as you could wish me, I assure you,' I said.

'A *productive*, useful mess,' interrupted Emellana.

'Quite. But I'm still hopelessly outclassed out here. Did we forget that part?'

'But,' said Emellana. 'We do have this.' And the damned lyre was back in her hands, its moonlit strings glittering in the rain.

'Woah.' I took two big steps backwards. 'I thought that was off-limits.'

'*Em*,' said Jay, scowling, and started towards her. 'We agreed—'

'We did,' she said, unruffled. 'But consider. This instrument has been soaking up magick ever since we arrived here. It is, at this time, far more powerful than it has ever been before, or likely will again. It almost overcame even me, when I wielded it just now. It is what we need. And who better to give it to than one whose peculiar affinity with the thing might just work in our favour?'

'And what about its effect on Ves?' Jay demanded.

Emellana looked at me. 'Have you ever played this lyre before?'

'No. No one would let me.' I signified my general agreement with this judgement by putting my hands behind my back. 'I don't think they were wrong, either.'

'Why is that?'

'Because just looking at it is enough to overset me.' I tried not to suit actions to words and gaze moonily at the pretty thing, and failed.

'So I see.' Emellana sat in thought, her fingers lightly stroking the moonsilver or skysilver or whatever it was that made up the lyre's graceful curves. 'I have heard of nothing that would account for that effect,' she said at last. 'I think, Cordelia Vesper, that it will have to come down to courage. You will not know what you can do with this lyre — or what it will do to you — until you try it.'

I attempted a smile, though my guts were churning. I can't explain what that thing does to me but I don't like it. 'An exciting new round of Trial and Error,' I said, with a glance at Jay.

He tried to smile, too, and failed. His dark eyes were worried. 'Are you up for it, Ves?'

'Addie's out there,' I said. 'I brought her here. I can't leave her here. If there's no other way...'

Emellana smiled faintly, serenely confident. 'I believe all will turn out well.'

'Oh, you do?' I said politely. 'That is a great comfort.' I swallowed, and added, 'Sorry. That was rude.'

I was surprised by the wide grin that swept over Emellana Rogan's face. 'Wonderfully,' she agreed.

'Right.' I stood straighter. 'We need to be fast. The dregs of those awful potions won't last us much longer. I don't know about you, but I can feel *crazy-insane Ves* creeping up on me with every passing half-hour. Mir?'

'Yes,' she said, appearing at my elbow.

'The griffins are your business. I'm hoping they'll be groggy and confused more than violently angry when we've broken them out, so you shouldn't be in too much danger, but... be careful. Right?'

'Right. I—' She broke off, biting her lip.

'What is it?'

'I don't know how to handle griffins. You've seen more of them than I have.'

'That's okay,' I said, with a bright, bright smile. 'None of us has any idea what we're doing.'

Her answering smile was sour. 'Excellent.'

'Welcome to my world. Though not quite. You know more about magickal beasts than anyone, and you've all the magick you need to help you. I may despise you at this time, but I know you can do this. Jay?'

'Right here.'

I sought out the flickering, pale shape of Adeline far above, and pointed. 'Addie. I'm going to bring her back down here somehow. Will you... catch her? Not literally,' I hastened to add.

He smiled faintly. 'I'll take care of her.'

'Thank you. And pup...' I had to chase to catch up with her, but I scooped her up, and gave her to Emellana. 'Keep her safe,' I said. 'Please.'

Emellana took a firm grip upon my wriggling pup. 'She will be well,' she promised.

'Great. Well.' I looked up at the sky, out over the darkening, drenched town, and finally at Jay. 'Here goes nothing?'

'You'll be okay,' he said, looking steadily at me.

I could have reminded him about the lengths he'd gone to to keep me away from the lyre, but that was a waste of time. 'Listen. If I end up as a plate of pancakes again, I'm relying on you to turn me back.'

'But you love pancakes.'

'And I'd prefer to remain a pancake-loving Ves than... a pancake.'

He smiled. 'I'll hang onto you.'

'Thanks.' I took a deep breath. I wasn't worried about pancakes, exactly, only the absolutely unpredictable effects of putting that lyre into my, of all, hands — and doing it out here, when we were magick-swamped already, and mad around the edges.

I'd make a mess, no doubt about that. And what would be left of me once I'd finished?

What would be left of Vale?

No time to worry about that now. Emellana was right; the only way to find out what would happen was to dive in.

'Lyre, please,' I said.

Emellana tucked Goodie under one arm. She beckoned strangely at a button on her shirt, which shone, and twisted, and became a tiny, rapidly-growing lyre. In another moment, she was holding out the real, full-sized thing to me.

'Nice glamour,' I said.

She inclined her head in grave acceptance of the compliment. 'It is one of my better arts.'

'I'd say so.' I steeled myself, and held out one hand to the dangerously beautiful instrument.

It called to me. My fingers itched as they neared the lyre, and then began to burn with a heat I found both abrasive and comforting.

The cursed thing began to shine with a light that was... purple. My very favourite shade thereof.

'You are so determined to seduce me,' I muttered, and with a deep breath I made a grab for it.

The gleaming silvery metal proved warm under my hands, soothing like a hearth-fire in winter — and terrifying, like a house-fire literally whenever.

And I, little Cordelia Vesper, went up like a torch.

19

HAVE YOU EVER BEEN played by a lyre? I'll wager not. I don't especially recommend it; at least, not by *this* specimen. If it must be so, try for a mild-mannered, grandmotherly type; the sort that will have you baking Victoria sponge cakes and puttering about in the garden.

Not the sort that will pump you full of all the magick it has been blithely soaking up until your nose bleeds. *Not* the sort that will use you and discard you like a sodding handkerchief.

When I took up that lyre, it was as though either I or it (or both) ceased to exist; instead of the-moonsilver-lyre or Vesper-Cordelia, there was simply a force. And while taking up the lyre had enhanced my mother's and Emellana's ability to track past magicks, or imbued one or the other of my parents with the ancient magick of faerie monarchy, in my case the effect was, um, different.

Forgive me if I sound deranged, for I doubtless was at that moment. In *my* case, the effect was to turn me into a magickal source all in my own self. I was, if you like, the human equivalent of a griffin or a unicorn.

I'd have laughed if I hadn't been so busy leaking blood.

The lyre all but fused to my fingers, so that I could hardly have let go of it if I'd wanted to. And for a few agonising seconds, I desperately did, for it *hurt*. The lyre-through-me drank up every drop of magick in the vicinity (did I properly emphasise that this is a *lot*?), and then poured it forth again in a veritable ocean — only stronger, and... changed.

I learned how it feels, when lightning arcs over a griffin's hide. I learned what it means. It is a discharge of magick, because there is too much of it to hold.

That hurts, too.

Vale lay spread before me, but I no longer saw it with my half-blind human eyes. I saw it as a pattern of magick; a map, if you like, of ancient power. I saw its centre: Mount Vale, and its colony of griffins. I saw pockets of intense magick dotted here and there; the unicorn farms, I judged, and the travel points, and other things I could not name. I saw its ebbs and flows, its strengths and its weaknesses.

Terrifying came the knowledge: I could have stretched out a hand and rearranged it like a chess board, if I had so chosen.

I didn't so choose. All I wanted was Adeline. I found her: a mote of bright magick, purer than her peers, and in some odd way familiar. Around her crackled a web of magick: a net to hold her in, and all those like her.

I plucked her free of it, and then unwound the net. It came free easily enough, though every strand of it burned and blistered and I shuddered with the pain of it. Grimly, I ripped it into tatters and let it stream away, watching with distant satisfaction as the ribbons of magick dissolved back into the flow around Mount Vale.

Motes of bright magick scattered around me as the mythical beasts of Vale fled the town, free.

'So that's good, then,' I said sleepily, looking wide-eyed up at the sky, for my shaking legs had long since found it impossible to hold me. The firmament was a spiral of magick, too, a shimmering, pulsing, coiling, glorious mass; even the clouds were laced through with it, pregnant with possibility.

I wondered, somewhere in my befuddled brain, whether our Britain looked at all the same.

I thought not.

'Ves,' someone said, but whoever it was must have been very far away. The wind took any words that followed, and I barely felt the hands that shook my shoulders.

I felt the teeth, though, that fastened onto my left wrist.

'Ouch,' I said, frowning, and looked vaguely about. Something bright and lovely was near me, contours of magick that were familiar and dear, for all their strangeness. I reached out my other hand to touch it, and felt warmth. 'Addie?'

'*Ves*,' said the voice again, and it came from a coil of intense magick near my shoulder. Not bright like Addie, this one, but like banked heat.

It shook me again.

'Mm,' I said.

'...the lyre,' said the voice, distant but urgent. 'Get the damned lyre off her!'

Another shifting something registered upon my senses: incandescent, this, in a muted way, like the sun behind a veil, and it glittered with such indescribable beauty that I was moved to tears.

'She's crying,' said the urgent voice. Jay's voice. Sense filtered, dimly, through.

'She will be all right,' said a dusty, aged, comforting voice, and Emellana's age-withered fingers gently extracted the lyre from my hands.

Agony tore through me: first my arms, as though I had plunged them into molten lava. Then the rest of my shrinking body, as though my organs had been torn free of me all in a rush, leaving me naught but a shell.

'*What have you done?*' yelled Jay.

'As you instructed,' said Emellana, and even then, even in the face of my near-total disintegration, she was as cool as a clear lake. 'She and the lyre are separating.'

'*Separating?*'

I winced, for Jay spoke at such volume — and such close proximity, apparently — that the words shot through my seared head like nails. 'Jay,' I croaked.

He stopped shouting abruptly. 'Ves? Are you all right?'

The magick was bleeding out of my vision, all the beauteous light and brightness and mystery leaking away, and my eyes filled with tears of mingled agony and loss. Through the watery film, I discerned the blurred figure of Jay bending over me: dark jacket, dark hair. Near him, a large mass of purple: Emellana.

'Addie,' I croaked. 'Get your teeth out of my arm.'

She squeezed a fraction harder for good measure, then let me go. The pain of it had not much registered, compared to the indescribable torment imposed upon me by the lyre. Nonetheless, with the latter ebbing I was grateful to be reprieved of the smaller pain imparted by the diamond-hard teeth of a unicorn. 'Thanks,' I sighed, and ran my aching fingers through her mane.

She bumped me with her nose.

'Are you all right?' Jay said again, and with the tears in remission I could discern features. Dark eyes, wild with fear, fixed upon me, and a sheen of sweat upon Jay's brow which told me he'd suffered almost as much as I had.

I thought about the question for a while.

'No,' I decided.

Jay sat back on his heels, and looked up at the sky — normal again, darkened and greyish and drizzly — with an expression of frustrated entreaty. 'What the hell just happened?' he said, looking again at me.

'Do you want to tell him?' I said to Emellana. I made some small effort to sit up, but finding it beyond the wasted strength of my aching muscles I permitted myself to slither back down to the ground.

'She dissolved the net,' said Emellana.

'I see that,' Jay said, and waved an arm wildly at the skies. They were, I distantly realised, empty of griffins, unicorns, or any other unusual creature. 'But that's not what *happened*, is it?'

I wondered how the events of the past… half hour? How long? Had looked to Jay. Not good. Not good at all.

'It is as Milady suspected,' said Emellana, with a crooked smile for me. 'When combined, your Cordelia Vesper and the lyre are a formidable team.'

'What?' said Jay, his brow snapping down.

'We're a font,' I said. 'Like a griffin.' I remembered the crackle of magick about me, and squinted down at my shirt and trousers. Were they singed?

They were.

I sighed.

'I thought the lyre absorbed magick,' said Jay. 'Wouldn't that make you a sponge, not a font?'

'We're both,' I said wearily. 'They're both. The griffins and such. That's how it works.'

'Put enough griffins into a place like Vale, already a source of strong magick, and the effects are profound,' said Emellana. 'They feed each other, you see.'

'I don't think I do,' Jay sighed. 'What I do see is an exhausted Ves who, as far as I can tell, almost died about ten minutes ago, and who urgently needs to be got out of here.'

'Wasn't dying,' I protested.

'Pardon me, but you sure looked like it,' said Jay. He was still wearing his worried face.

'Wasn't dying,' I repeated firmly. 'I was… changing.'

'Into what?'

I sighed and sat up again. This time, the world did not revolve around me quite so much, and I was able to maintain the posture. 'I don't know.'

Truth. I could not say what had become of me; only I felt, all the way down to my bones, that I was not quite the same Ves anymore. That will happen to a girl, when you channel half an ocean of magick through her insides.

'Milady,' I said, as some of Emellana's words filtered through to my weary brain. 'Suspected? What?'

Emellana gave me that crooked smile again. 'You heard me.'

'How could she suspect?' I said.

'On what possible evidence?' Jay added. 'And why wouldn't she *just tell us.*'

I laid a hand over Jay's, detecting signs of an imminent melt-down. 'You'll get used to Milady.'

'But do I want to?'

Fair question. I couldn't answer it.

'She had no evidence,' said Emellana, getting slowly to her feet. 'It is more that she has... what might once have been termed "hunches".'

'And how do you know that?' I said, eyeing our enigmatic assistant with some suspicion.

Emellana only shrugged. 'I am old, and so is she. There has been time enough.'

'For what?'

'A great many things.' She squinted out over the horizon, her back turned to me, and said: 'I believe we are shortly to encounter trouble.'

I swore. Of *course* we were. If I'd had even half my wits about me I would have anticipated as much, for having just torn their intricate, powerful and surprisingly-not-that-old net of magick to bits, it ought to have occurred to me that someone would swiftly become aware of it. The circling motes of magickal energy that had been the enslaved mythical beasts were gone, and... we were still there.

'Hup,' I said, hoping that the word might prove a bit magickal in its own way, and help me to find my feet.

It did not, but Jay did. He grabbed my arms and hauled me, gently but firmly, upright. He then proceeded to prop me up when I threatened to fall over again, though I noticed a pronounced sway in his own stance, and that sign about his eyes that suggested imminent trouble.

Oh, yes. We were still potion-free and increasingly magick-drunk, too.

Rarely have I had the privilege to preside over so disastrous a mission, and that's saying something. I am, after all, Princess Chaos.

'Erm,' I said intelligently. Was it my imagination or had I grown a tail?

I checked.

I had. Fittingly, it was a horse's tail, or perhaps by preference a unicorn's.

'Better move along,' Jay said. 'Can you walk?'

'Where's Mir?' To my shame, our erstwhile beast-mistress's entire existence had slipped my mind during all the excitement. Worse, I had about forgotten pup, too.

'That way,' said Jay, pointing with a jerk of his chin. 'She was pretty busy with those escaped griffins.'

Right. Of course. I had given her rather a lot of work to do.

I risked a look over my shoulder, and detected a glimpse of a human figure some way off, blonde hair whipping in the wind, a tiny golden ball of fluff dancing along at her heels.

Before me, the slope of Mount Vale stretched down and down. I did not waste much time watching for the approach of danger; they would use the same "lift" we had, er, "enjoyed", and come out right behind us.

'Em, can you think of another way off this hill?' I said.

'Not immediately.' When even Emellana Rogan showed faint signs of worry, well, that was about time for the rest of us to panic.

And I hadn't forgotten how the Court-at-Mandridore's emissary had appeared while the lyre and I had been making a magickal torch of ourselves.

'By the way,' I said. 'Just how old are you?'

'Another time,' she said curtly.

Did that mean *ask me later* or *I come from another age*?

Too late to wonder, for a shout went up behind us, and a stream of people poured onto the hilltop, stepping, seemingly, out of thin air. There were at least twenty of them; they were of a mixture of human, troll, and other fae races I could not at that moment name; they were universally angry; and one of them was Wyr.

'I want that case back!' I yelled, pointing at the latter.

'Well, and the good people of Vale were hoping not to lose their griffin carousel,' said Wyr. 'It seems we are all in for a disappointment today.' No trace of his earlier sardonic humour remained; the look he directed at us was ugly.

I glanced left. Miranda was circling around to reach us, my pup in her arms.

'How about we take that unicorn as payment?' said Wyr, advancing upon us, his happy little lynch-mob at his back.

'Ideas?' I said desperately.

Emellana shook her head.

Jay, though, began to rummage furiously in his pockets. 'The thing,' he said, helpfully.

'The what?'

'Orlando's thing. You know!'

Ohhh, the *thing*. The nameless-but-potent thing Orlando had put into our hands. The untried-and-only-sort-of-tested thing that might award us just the stroke of luck we needed to survive the day.

Or it might land us at the bottom of the ocean. I mean, if Orlando didn't know, who did?

Nonetheless. 'I've got it,' I said, and stuck my hand in my shoulder bag.

'Oof,' said Mauf.

'Sorry,' I gasped. My fingers closed over the smooth, cool disc of something and I drew it out.

'Next problem,' I said, gazing at it in perfect incomprehension. 'How does it work?'

Wyr-and-company were closing on us; Miranda was too far away to reach us in time; and I had no clue how to operate our panic button.

Did I use the word *disaster* before? I think I did.

'Right,' I said. 'Addie, fetch Mir. Jay, Em, take a deep breath.'

The next article to exit my trusty shoulder-bag was my Sunstone Wand. I tossed Orlando's toy into the air, levelled my Wand at it, and shot a blast of pure magick high into the sky.

It hit the clear disc in a shower of sparks, and the world exploded.

20

'I'M A BUTTERFLY,' I said in wonder.

No, I didn't. I tried to speak, but seeing as I was lacking the right mouth parts, nothing much emerged.

I was also wrong, as soon became apparent, for no butterfly had gnarly, greeny-browny, webby toes and a fierce hunger for fresh, juicy flies.

'I'm a toad,' I said. 'With wings.' No words emerged that time either, but my tongue did. It went a long, long way out, and returned with a fly stuck to its tip.

I didn't want to swallow that fly, but I did.

Yuck.

Pros to the situation: me and my bosom companions (and Miranda) were no longer pinned at the edge of the hilltop of Mount Vale, a steep drop behind us and an angry mob before us. We were airborne; soaring through the dulcet skies; wafted upon wings wrought of Orlando's weird magick. (Did it *have* to be a toad, Orlando? Really?)

The cons? Those same dreamy skies happened to be filled with a swarm of griffins, recently released from slavery and absolutely hopping mad.

'*Orlando!*' I screamed (in my head) as I ducked the advances of the nearest griffin, tumbling head-over-wings in my haste to escape its snapping beak. Boy, do those things look big when you're that small. '*This is not my idea of good luck!*' I only belatedly recalled that Orlando hadn't said anything about good luck. The word he had used had been *chaos*.

To say the least.

I risked a glance around, first chance I got, and was not reassured. A wooden bucket full of soapy water drifted past me; had to be one of us, surely, but who? Jay, Em or Mir? At least they weren't edible. On my other side, though, was an oversized fairy cake, unusually buoyant, and doubtlessly delicious; and beyond that, a small memorandum book, covers flapping like wings, its pages rapidly turning damp and soggy in the never-ending drizzle.

The bucket up-ended itself, pouring its load of soap and water out onto the ground far below. Then it darted in my direction, and scooped me up.

I fell into the bucket's depths with a *plop*.

All right, so I couldn't see a thing, and had to just trust that the bucket was the current shape of someone I knew and trusted. But! Woodish bucket walls are griffin-proof.

I permitted myself a small sigh of relief — and narrowly avoided a squashing as the fairy cake hurtled down upon me from above, followed by the memorandum book.

Looking at the former, I became painfully aware of gnawing hunger. When was the last time we had remembered to eat? And look at the thing! Fat, curvaceous, positively drowning in icing that smelled of peaches—

'Ves?' said the book, somehow, but it was addressing the cake, not the winged toad.

I mean, of course it was. If I'd had a choice, I would have gone for the cake, and never mind the consequences.

Griffins probably don't even like cake, anyway.

I made some small attempt at a response, but that being as successful as my earlier efforts I gave up, and sat catching my breath while the book did its level best to engage the cake in conversation.

...Did I just say that?

Our adventures don't get any more sensible, do they?

Some little time later, our courteous bucket-escort made a graceful dive, and carefully emptied us all out onto the ground again. There was grass under me, my exquisitely sensitive toes were quick to discern, but more than that I could not have said. The world was too big to admit of greater detail; everything beyond about three inches distant was a vague, green blur.

We sat there, the bucket, the book, the cake and I, and waited.

It was Jay who regained his usual form first. He'd been the bucket, not much to my surprise. I knew it was Jay, because the grass before my nose was abruptly obscured by a bluish haze I recognised after a moment as denim. Jay's leg, encased in jeans.

'Hi,' I didn't quite say.

Jay squinted down at us. 'Ves?' he said.

He was talking to the cake.

I waved a leg at him, and stuck out my tongue.

In another moment I was Ves-shaped-and-sized again, and having not had the sense to back up before my sudden transformation I found myself practically in Jay's lap when it happened.

'Ahem,' I said, scooting backwards. 'Welcome back, Mr. Bucket.'

'At least it was practical,' he said, frowning at me.

'I had wings! It could have been worse. I could have been a flying fairy cake.'

Both of us looked at the cake, and then the book, wondering which was which.

I tell you what, if the cake had turned out to be Miranda I might have gutted her on the spot for the pure insult of it all.

Fortunately for her, the cake wriggled and wiggled and exploded into Emellana.

Two minutes later, the memorandum book (having sat impatiently shuffling its pages for some time) became Miranda, and there we were. She still had the pup in her arms, to my relief (what had Goodie been in this scenario, the bookmark...? I abandoned the question as it made my brain hurt).

'Where's Addie?' I said, seized by sudden panic.

Everyone looked wildly around, but no one came back with a response.

I remembered Wyr's final words. *How about we take that unicorn as payment?* I had last seen her racing in Miranda's direction, but what if Wyr had somehow intercepted her?

'Hang on,' said Jay, looking hard at Miranda (who lay prone, white with exhaustion and virtually insensible. I smothered a faint twinge of pity laced with guilt, for who had given her the task of shepherding all those griffins to freedom? Me, that's who). Jay reached over and touched the shoulder of Miranda's jumper. I detected the glint of metal.

It was a pin badge, the kind certain people wear on flat-caps. This one, though, was a tiny, dancing unicorn.

'That's not mine,' said Miranda, frowning in puzzle-ment.

'Let me have it,' I said.

Mir carefully detached the badge, and dropped it into my hand. It lay in my palm, inert.

I put it on the ground, and took out my pipes.

'Quickly, Ves,' said Jay. 'We need to be gone.'

I nodded. He didn't have to tell me. We may have evaded Wyr and his lynch-mob but it wouldn't take them long to figure out where we must be. Jay had taken us straight back to the henge-point through which we'd first arrived — courtesy of Wyr.

I played Adeline's song on my little skysilver pipes — and suffered a severe shock. The music rang out, impossibly loud, amplified in both volume and magick beyond anything reasonable. Magick vibrated in my bones, shimmered behind my eyes, and gave me a blinding headache.

The badge at my feet didn't so much melt back into Adeline's warm, live shape as erupt into it. I was lucky I didn't blow her to bits with my magick.

I stopped playing, and stuffed the pipes back into my bra, trying to look nonchalant.

No such luck. Jay, Emellana and Miranda were staring at me like I'd grown a second head.

Giddy gods, what if I *had?*

I checked. Just the one head.

All right, then.

'So are we going?' I said, and gestured towards the stone circle that stood quietly awaiting our getting our act together. I leaned carefully upon Addie, hoping it would look like affection and not like my knees were trembling so badly I knew I would fall over.

'That tail you had is gone,' said Jay, staring still at me. 'And the flowers in your hair.'

'And the hay,' said Emellana.

She and I looked at each other. Emellana, ancient beyond reason and somehow unaffected by the magick of Vale.

And me, a spring chicken by her standards, but so overflowing with magick that Vale could no longer touch me.

'It's been an interesting day,' I said.

Emellana's smile was wry. 'Let's get these two out of here,' she said.

Great thinking, for Jay's eyes had turned gold (I hadn't wanted to mention it), and Miranda, having slowly but steadily shrunk for the past ten minutes, looked likely to turn into a spriggan before my very eyes.

'Are you okay to drive?' I asked Jay.

He narrowed his weird, bright golden eyes at me, only now they were smoky-silver and swirling like clouds. 'Why wouldn't I be?'

'Because you're... never mind. Let's just go.'

A SHORT, TURBULENT WHILE later, we were back in Scarborough, trudging down the hill from the henge-complex. Night had fallen with a crash, and Jay's eyes really stood out in the darkness, I can tell you. They ceased gleaming after a while, though, and Mir regained her usual size. We were fine.

I, though, was still fizzing with magick. Outside of Vale, I noticed it rather more.

It itched.

'I wonder,' said I, halfway down the hill, 'if Orlando has more of those panic buttons.'

'I can't say that the toad shape quite suited you,' said Jay.

'I can ask him for an adjustment.'

Miranda said nothing. I looked sideways at her without seeming to, noting the wan look of her, and her stumbling walk. Emellana, unruffled still, was visibly flagging, and Jay had the grim expression and purposeful walk of a man too dog-tired to dare let it show. Even Addie walked with drooping nose, her hoofs clicking softly on the pavement, and the pup had fallen asleep in Miranda's arms long ago.

I knew how they felt, because I had felt the same an hour or two ago.

But that was before.

Now I felt fine. Now, I felt *great.* I was overflowing with energy, buzzing with purpose, lively beyond all conceivable reason, and my hunger was gone. I, Cordelia Vesper, hadn't eaten all day and I didn't want a thing. Not even a pancake.

Something was deeply wrong.

'You okay, Ves?' said Jay after a while.

I curtailed the jauntiness of my walk, and slowed my steps to match his. 'Fine!' I carolled.

'I can see that.'

I felt rather than saw him exchanging a look with Emellana.

'We'll need food and sleep,' I said briskly — remembering to say *we* instead of *you.*

'We need to go home,' said Jay.

'What? No! We aren't finished here. We still haven't found out what became of Torvaston and Co, and what about the scroll-case?'

'Later,' said Jay. 'We need to go home.'

'But we're fine. A solid night's sleep and a hot meal—'

'Ves,' Jay interrupted. 'You look like you could run a marathon at a sprint, climb Mount Vale, swim the channel and still be ready for more. Forgive me, but that is not like you.'

'I—'

'Ves.'

'Yes?'

Jay stopped walking, and took my arm, forcing me to stop too. 'You're not fine.'

I swallowed. 'I'll be all right.'

'Once we get you home. We need to find out just what the lyre did, and... mend the effects.'

'You know what the lyre did. I told you.'

'Turned you into some kind of human griffin? That doesn't even make sense.'

'Think of me as a power source. Like a battery.'

Jay grimaced. 'Because that doesn't sound broken at all.'

'I'm not broken.'

'Can we just go home, and sort this out? We can come back, and finish the mission later.'

Jay had stopped us on a street corner. They didn't have street lamps in this version of Britain; light simply emanated from nowhere in particular, softly illuminating the cobblestones and aged brick around us — and Jay's worried face, looking down at me. 'Miranda and Emellana need some proper attention, too,' he said. 'And it's probably not safe for Addie to stay here for much longer, what with everyone after her majestic hide.'

'All perfectly true,' I conceded. 'So then, why don't you take Addie and the ladies home, and I'll wait for you here?'

'How in hell does that make sense? Are you just being difficult, Ves, because I swear I'll—'

'I'm not being difficult,' I said, cutting him off mid-rant. 'At least, not on purpose. The thing is, I...' I paused, and waited while a stout lady hastened past, an umbrella contraption floating along over her head. 'I don't think I can go home,' I said in a small voice.

'You don't think you *can*?'

I nodded, my throat dry. 'It... I felt all right, in Vale. Not... overcharged. The farther we get from Vale, the more overloaded I feel. Jay... our Britain is a magickal backwater compared to here. Remember what the woman in the elixir shop said?'

'I remember.' His voice was very grim.

I tried to smile. 'I'm calibrated for Vale right now, if not more. Until it wears off, I daren't go home for fear I'll... explode. Or something.'

'Or something.'

I shrugged. 'Explode; warp everything I touch into winged toads or talking cakes or the gods-know-what; spend the rest of my days as a plate of pancakes; I don't even *know* what will happen, only I'm pretty sure I don't get to waltz Home and have a cosy chat with Milady, followed by a nice cup of chocolate. I'm stuck, Jay.'

He looked long at me, and I couldn't read whatever thoughts were passing behind his (thankfully normal again) eyes. At length, he nodded. 'I'm staying with you, then. Emellana can—'

'I stay, too,' she said, firmly.

Jay nodded again. 'Very well. Miranda?'

She blinked vaguely at us, and I wondered how much she was even comprehending in her sleep-addled state. 'Just let me sleep for twelve or fourteen hours, and I'm ready for anything.'

Adeline bumped me from behind, her nose velvet-soft against my neck. I wasn't sure whether this was intended as a gesture of support or an objection, but I decided to take it as the former.

'So, we go on,' I said. 'We've lost the scroll-case, but we have Mauf's copy of the map.'

'To the mountains, then?' said Jay.

I nodded. 'To Hyndorin — and, it's to be hoped, Torvaston.'

'And maybe along the way, we'll figure out how to fix you.' Jay gave me the confident, bracing smile of a man with faint hopes.

Later, I sat wide awake in an armchair while three people and a puppy slept deeply around me. We'd had money enough for a single room, and an extra set of blankets. Jay lay wrapped in the latter at my feet; Emellana and Miranda had the twin beds. The place was scant, sparse and comfortless, but it hardly mattered. In the morning we'd be gone, far over the country to the Hyndorin Mountains, and whatever horrors or delights awaited us there.

For me, though, sleep would not come. I sat curled up and shivering, chockful of magick, watching with idle interest as the chair warped and curled around me, and waited for morning.

Also By Charlotte E. English

Modern Magick

The Road to Farringale

Toil and Trouble

The Striding Spire

The Fifth Britain

Royalty and Ruin

Music and Misadventure

The Wonders of Vale

The Heart of Hyndorin

223

House of Werth